DOUBLE BOSSED

TAKEN BOOK 1

KL RAMSEY

AIRIANA

Airiana Scott watched as her brother-in-law, Holden Kade passed by her new boss's office and gave her a smile and a wave. She was so grateful to him for helping her land the secretarial position at his firm a few months back. Airi loved that she and her son, Milo, got to live in the same town as her big sister, Ivy. She was excited about the fact she was going to be around when Ivy, Holden and Slade decided to have a little one of their own. Judging from her sister's little belly and her growing aversion to alcohol, she was pretty sure Ivy was going to be a mommy very soon. The thought of having a little niece or nephew around to spoil, made her giddy. She also loved that Milo would have a little cousin to run around with. But, being around Ivy's happy family came with pangs of jealousy and longing for something she was never sure she would have. Milo's father wanted nothing to do with either of them and honestly, they were better off for it. Her loser ex wasn't someone she wanted in her life and she certainly didn't want him in her son's life.

Cole Summers took off after Ivy, Slade and Holden found her and she knew he'd done her a favor disappearing from her life. Her sister tried to get her to track him down, to go after him for child support but it would open the door for Cole to see his son, and she wasn't sure that would be a good idea. Airi wanted to make it on her own, not only for herself but for her son. She owed him that much as his mother. Milo didn't ask to have an asshole for a father or be born to a single mother but this was his life. She just hoped she could make it better for him because Milo deserved the best of her—from her.

When Ivy and the guys first found Airi living with Cole, she wasn't sure how she felt about Ivy being in an open poly relationship. She worried her sister had been brain washed into a lifestyle which wasn't right for her. But seeing just how much the three of them loved each other, needed and took care of each other, made her long to find someone to share her life with. First, it would help if she could get some semblance of her life together, and then maybe find a guy to date. Still, it would feel damn good to at least be on the right track. Any man she dated would have to accept she had an almost one-year old son and at her age, a man like that would be hard to find. Most guys in their twenties didn't want to be tied down to an instant family and that was exactly what she was. They were a package deal and the few dates she had been on, since having Milo and moving to town, were disasters. Once the guy she was out with asked about her personal life and she shared she was a single mother, they would come up with some lame excuse to cut the date short.

At least they didn't waste her time trying to get in her pants; she had that to be thankful for. Airi decided not to date for a while. She wanted to really settle into her new job and she had enough going on, getting Milo accustomed to his new daycare and starting her search for a bigger place for them to live. She was thankful her new company had a great in-house daycare and she could visit Milo on her breaks and lunch, which was a huge bonus. Ivy's boss, Cash, let her and Milo crash in the apartment above his bar and she was grateful she had a place to call her own. She and Milo were cramped and had to share a bedroom but for now, it worked. Airi hoped to save enough money to get herself a nice little house in town but it would take some time. Ivy offered to help but she had already done so much for her and Milo, there was no way she could accept her sister's generous offer. Besides, a part of her liked the idea of making it on her own. It was time for her to grow up and learn to fend for herself.

When Airi thought Ivy had gotten out of the foster care system and just left her, she felt lost and hopeless. She really didn't care where she ended up and with whom, that was why she let Cole hurt her for so long. Airiana didn't feel she was worthy of better and that was something she was working on. She was seeing a therapist, once a week, to work on her self-esteem issues and her anger over being abused. Mainly, she was mad at herself for letting someone do that to her but she had some anger towards Ivy and her parents, along with the typical abandonment issues from being left. Airi knew she was eventually going to have to work through all the tough issues but for now, it was nice to have someone to talk to, even if she was paying her therapist to listen. She would do whatever it took to be the best mom she could be for Milo.

Starting her new job was a fresh beginning for her. Airi's bosses were great and it didn't hurt that they were sexy as sin. Jarrod and Justin Grayson were the owners of Grayson Industries, and were sought after by businesses and women alike. Besides being one of the top fortune five hundred companies in the world, they were both wealthy, eligible bachelors who made the local women in town completely gaga. Airi had to admit, she could see the appeal. They were both hot as hell and her main job was to keep out the unwanted attention. She spent her mornings opening the guys "fan mail", which usually consisted of panties and love letters, dripping with perfume and naughty suggestions. She read a few and had to admit they made her blush but most everything did anyway. Every day, Jarrod and Justin would make a big deal of throwing the letters and trinkets into the garbage, unfazed by the unwanted attention. The guys seemed to be oblivious to the fact they were garnering so much attention, more fixated on their company than conquests. Although, she did overhear Ivy and Holden talking about her bosses joining Pandora's Box. That fact shouldn't surprise her though, since they did lend Cash and Slade the money to start the BDSM club. Airi imagined it had to be hard for either of her sexy bosses to meet women outside of the gold digger fan club, which seemed to gather in their lobby on a daily basis.

Airi peeked into Jarrod's office to find him sitting behind his desk staring at his computer screen and she almost hated to interrupt him. Jarrod was the more intense brother; Justin was easier going and even flirty but she was sure he was like that with all women. In the last few months, Justin had taken her to lunch or showed up at her desk with takeout every day. She felt like she was monopolizing his time but she had come to cherish their daily chats and time together.

As if on cue, Justin showed up with a smile on his face and from the delicious aromas coming from the bag, Asian takeout. "Yum," she hummed. She couldn't think of anything better to cure a case of the Monday's then noodles with one of her hot bosses.

"I take it Asian is alright, then?" Justin cocked his eyebrow at her and the way he looked her up and down, waiting for her response had her squirming in her seat.

"Asian is perfect, as long as you tell me there is Pho in that bag," she said. Justin's smile told her she had guessed correctly and he pulled up a chair to her desk. He sat so close to her their legs touched, causing her to feel a little overheated. Justin paying her any attention had her overly active imagination dreaming of him offering her more than just lunch dates. Airi needed to remember he was just showing her kindness and helping her to get settled in her new role. Most of their lunches involved him showing her how to run the numerous systems they required her to understand. She really had no experience, so Justin had taken it upon himself to train her as his and Jarrod's personal assistant. Airi knew the score—they hired her because of her brother-in-law Holden, working for them and she would do anything not to let him or them down. She needed this job, not just for herself but for her son.

As if he could read her thoughts, Justin asked about Milo and she couldn't hide her smile. Thinking about her little guy always made her perk up. He was such a happy baby, she couldn't imagine her life without him, no matter how hard being a single mother was.

"He's good," she gushed. "I ran upstairs to the daycare center to check on him during my morning break."

Justin nodded, "I feel badly about keeping you from him during our work lunches. If you want to take a few extra breaks during the day to check on him, we'd understand." Airi looked past Justin into where Jarrod was still hard at work. The man never seemed to take breaks, not even for lunch. She found it hard to think of him as being as understanding as Justin about her running up to check in on Milo.

"I'm good," she whispered. "You both have already been so accommodating when it comes to working with me and my schedule. I don't want to take advantage of your generosity." Airiana knew she was lucky to find a company with such lax policies about bringing children to work. She never dreamt she'd find someplace like Grayson Industries to work for and she didn't want to push her luck.

"Well, the offer stands, if you would like to have more time with him. I was just up there myself and he seems so happy playing with the other kids." Airi gasped, not hiding her surprise at Justin's words.

"You were up checking on Milo?" She asked. Justin smiled and nodded.

"He kind of grows on you after a while, doesn't he?" Justin admitted. "Besides, I love kids and I try to run up to the daycare just to check on everyone. It really brightens my day. I almost wish I could spare an hour or two just to sit and play with them. Their lives are so simple, I need more of that," Justin said. He looked back over his shoulder to where his brother worked and Airi didn't miss the sadness in his eyes. She couldn't help herself; she reached across her desk and covered his hand with hers. Justin looked down at her hand, and Airi instantly regretted being so forward, pulling hers back.

"I'm sorry," she whispered. "I shouldn't have done that. It was very forward of me." Justin smiled at her and reached across her desk, taking her hand into his own.

"Not forward at all, Airi," he said. "You just surprised me."

Airi looked down to where their hands were joined and wasn't sure if she should push but she had so many questions when it came to her bosses. Most of them were too personal to ask but she wanted to push her luck, just a little.

"You sometimes seem so sad when you look at your brother, Justin," she almost whispered.

Justin put his fork down and started to clean up his lunch, causing Airi to instantly regret her statement. She wished she could take her words back but it was too late for that. She was screwing up their whole lunch.

"I'm sorry, Justin," she apologized. She reached over to touch his arm and he flinched. "I, um I-" she stammered, wishing she could just hide. "I need to run to the ladies room, please excuse me." Airi stood and hurried past him to the executive washrooms. She found the ladies room empty and breathed a sigh of relief, slinking back against the wall.

"I'm a fucking idiot," she said, covering her face with her hands. She didn't want to cry, while standing in the middle of the ladies room but once the flood gates broke, there was no stopping her tears. Airi wiped at her face. She wouldn't allow herself to break down now. She needed to get herself together and get back to her desk. Hopefully, Justin would just forget she was an idiot and they could move past her saying inappropriate personal things to him. If not, she always had the ladies room to hide away in.

JUSTIN

Justin watched as Airi ran off, saying she had to use the ladies room. He knew he had fucked things up during their lunch together and he hated how he made her feel uncomfortable. Hell, she had him pegged and he wasn't quite sure how to react to her astute conclusions about he and Jarrod's relationship lately. In the past few months his twin brother had pushed him away and it hurt like hell.

Things between them seemed to go downhill after they agreed to hire Holden Kade's sister-in-law. Their new, sexy assistant seemed to turn both of their heads and when he admitted to Jarrod he wanted her; his brother shut him out. He became obsessed with work and even stopped going out to the local club they had helped to fund, Pandora's Box, to have a little fun and blow off some steam. Justin had to admit he wasn't as interested in finding a pretty little sub to spend his time with since meeting Airi but his brother had shut himself off from everything except work.

Justin wished Jarrod would let him in, just tell him what was eating at him. If he knew his brother, like he thought he did, Justin would guess his brother wanted Airi just as much as he did and didn't know what to do about it.

He had even caught Jarrod up at the daycare center, playing with little Milo a few times and he usually grumbled out something about just liking kids and walked away. Justin worried their attraction to Airi was going to drive a wedge between them, and he would never let that happen. He would walk away from her before he'd lose his brother; he just wished Jarrod could see that.

Jarrod appeared in the doorway. The walls were literally made of glass, so he was sure his brother had witnessed the whole exchange between he and Airi. He was sure most of their floor was now talking about how he had made his poor assistant so upset she had to run to the bathroom just to escape him.

"What happened to Airiana?" Jarrod asked. He looked angry but he didn't give that away with his carefree tone. Justin knew his brother well enough to know when he was upset or even angry, like now.

"I kind of fucked up and upset her," Justin admitted.

"What the fuck did you do to her?" Jarrod asked, finally showing his hand.

"I didn't do anything," Justin barked back. He sighed, knowing it wasn't entirely true. "Fuck," he growled. "Airi made an observation about me and it hit a little too close to home, so I acted like an ass," he admitted.

"What was the observation?" Jarrod asked.

"She said I seem a little sad when it comes to you," Justin whispered. He didn't want to draw any more unwanted attention from the office gossips. They seemed to come out of the woodwork whenever he and Jarrod got into a heated conversation and usually, by the next day, rumors were circulating that they were closing Grayson Industries and laying everyone off. Theatrics ran high around the office and he didn't want to have to deal with anymore HR meetings and reassure everyone that their jobs were safe.

"Sad? Why would she say that?" Jarrod feigned ignorance but he knew exactly what was going on between the two of them. Justin was just more sensitive about these things than Jarrod would ever let on being.

"You know exactly what she means, Jarrod. Things haven't been the same with us since I admitted to liking Airi. You feel the same way about her but you're just too chicken to admit it. It's alright if we both want her," Justin dramatically whispered.

Jarrod shook his head, "You don't get it, brother. What good would come from us both falling for the same woman? Sure, we share women but falling for the same one would only drive us apart and I won't have that. She's only twenty-two years old and I'm pretty sure we just celebrated our thirty-fifth birthdays, which makes her much too young for either of us. Plus, there's the fact she works for us and HR would have a fucking field day with us dating an employee. I don't want Airiana," he shouted. His eyes darted past where Justin stood, at Airi's desk, and Jarrod closed his eyes and groaned.

"Shit," Justin said, knowing she was standing just behind him before he even turned around to check. He turned to find Airi's tear-stained face and it nearly did him in. Her face was a beautiful, angry mask and she looked as if she could strangle his brother. Honestly, Justin felt the same way about Jarrod at this point. Not only was his brother denying his feelings, now he was being a complete ass and hurting Airi.

"I'm so sorry, Airi," Justin said. "Jarrod didn't mean-"

"I meant every word, Justin. Don't put words into my mouth. I'm sorry if I upset you, Airiana," Jarrod barked. He nodded as if dismissing her and turned to go into his office. Jarrod frosted his windows, effectively shutting them both out and Airi brushed past Justin to take her seat.

"If you'll excuse me, Justin, I have a ton of work to get back to," Airi said. Justin watched as she rearranged her desk, tossing out half her lunch. He wanted to tell her he was sorry. Hell, he wanted to pull her up from her fucking chair and crush her against his body but that wouldn't help his case. He had messed up, big time. Justin worried he wouldn't be able to fix things between them and that made him feel desperate to try.

"Airi," he paused when she shot him a look that told him she was in no mood to discuss anything further. "I'm sorry," he whispered and retreated into his office. He had spent all these months trying to get close to his assistant and one fucked up conversation with Jarrod sent all his good intentions down the drain. Justin didn't want to hurt his brother but he was afraid he wouldn't be able to turn off wanting Airi. He just didn't know what to do next but he'd have to come up with something fast, because losing either of them wasn't an option.

JARROD

Jarrod spent the next fucking week running damage control with his sexy personal assistant. There was nothing he could do to make her forget he was an ass, blurting out that he didn't want her when she was all he could think about, day and night. He had gone to Pandora's Box, the BDSM club he and Justin were members at, trying to find a sub to help him forget the way Airiana looked at him. Each night, he left the club with a burning ache he was sure would never be satisfied. Airiana's big blue eyes showed every emotion she was keeping bottled up, including the betrayal of him being an arrogant asshole and pushing her away. There was no way he'd go after her now, knowing his brother wanted her too.

Jarrod knew Justin was hoping he would admit to having feelings for their pretty assistant but what good would it do either of them? He would never challenge his brother over a woman. It was their unwritten bro code and not even someone as desirable as Airiana would have him changing his stance on the matter. Jarrod found out that morning about an upcoming business trip that would take him away from the office for the next few days, and he was looking forward to the break. He needed some alone time and that especially meant from his twin brother. They were just not connecting anymore and he knew that had everything to do with their sexy personal assistant. When he agreed to hire her, Jarrod never imagined they would both end up wanting her. He missed the signs but looking back now, he should have noticed the way his brother looked at Airiana. Maybe he didn't want to see them, because then he would have had to admit he wanted her just as much.

Now, this whole problem between he and Justin was because he hired their new assistant based on his own desire for her and not to fill the damn job. Sure, Airiana had become a valuable member of their company and in truth, she was so much more capable than her job description but telling her so would mean that eventually she would move on and he wouldn't be able to see her every day. Jarrod was sure he must be a masochist with the way he liked seeing her sitting outside of his office, day after day. Airiana had become the reason he got out of bed every morning, looking forward to going into work and the reason he was sad about having to go home every evening. Hell, he even liked her kid and that was something he never dreamed of happening. He was caught sneaking up to the daycare center on site just to check in on Milo on more than one occasion. He'd always brush it off as him just wanting to make sure his new assistant and her son were fitting into the company but it was so much more. Admitting that wouldn't end well for the three of them and he just needed to remember that every time Airiana looked at him with those soulful blue eyes of hers.

Jarrod had gotten into the office early, as he had everyday this past week and his twin seemed to be in a perpetual bad mood. Jarrod noticed Justin had stopped having lunches with Airiana and that pissed him off. He knew Justin was better suited for Airiana, even though the thought of having to watch the two of them together was excruciating. He would never begrudge his brother's happiness, no matter what his personal feelings were for their assistant.

The adjoining door, which separated their offices, swung open and Justin didn't bother with pleasantries. "Did you hear about the issues at the Colorado office?" Justin questioned. Jarrod had unfortunately been woken by a very early morning phone call from their manager at that office, detailing all the problems he was going to have to fly out there to fix.

"Yes," he confirmed. "I got the call from Maria this morning and I've already told her I will be there some time tomorrow."

Justin nodded, "Well, I've told her the same thing, basically. I guess we are flying to Colorado then."

"There is no need for us both to go," Jarrod said. He hated wasting resources and having them both fly to

Colorado, when one of them could easily handle the issues was a waste.

"Really, I think it might be good for us to get away for a few days. We've both been on edge and honestly, I miss you man." Jarrod hated admitting he felt the same way but he'd be lying if he said he didn't agree with his brother. They hadn't been in sync for months now but Jarrod was hoping to fix everything by taking some time away from the office, and hopefully giving Justin some one-on-one time with Airiana. But, maybe Justin was right. A few days away, just the two of them, might be good for putting things right between them again.

Jarrod nodded, "Fine, have the jet ready for noon and we can head out then, if that works for you," he said. Justin's smile was the first Jarrod had seen from him in over a week.

"Will do, thanks, Jarrod." Justin quickly made his way back to his own office and shut the door. Jarrod checked his watch, noting he had just a few hours to get packed and to the hanger. They were afforded many luxuries in life and private jets were just one of the perks of owning their own corporation. Jarrod shot off a few emails, letting everyone know he and Justin would be out of town for most of the week and decided to head back to his apartment to pack his bag.

He knew he was being a coward but working the rest of the morning from home would give him some much needed time away from Airiana and hopefully some perspective. Jarrod saw she wasn't at her desk, so he sent her an email telling her he'd be out the rest of the morning and to forward his calls. A part of him was happy he was going to be able to sneak out of the office without having to face her knowing stare and the other part of him—the part that lacked self-preservation—wished he'd get a chance to say goodbye to her before leaving on his trip.

AIRIANA

Justin called Airi into his office to go over his itinerary for his impromptu business trip to Colorado. She hated admitting that having the office to herself for the next few days wasn't an upsetting prospect. Ever since Jarrod blurted out he wasn't interested in her, the two of them were walking on eggshells around her and Airi was beginning to tire of their behavior.

Airi grabbed her tablet and her way into Justin's office, noticing he was wearing her favorite suit. She loved when he wore his charcoal gray pin striped suit. He always looked sexy but when he wore that suit, his blue eyes stood out—almost as if calling to her. She sat on the sofa in front of his desk ready to take notes, to make sure she was prepared for the week ahead.

"First, let me say that I'm sorry I haven't been around much, for our lunches, Airi." She wasn't sure what to say to his admission. Airi had spent most of last week worried she had done something wrong to piss

Justin off. Sure, telling him he seemed sad every time he was around his brother probably wasn't the best thing to say during their last lunch together. She overstepped and she hated how he seemed so angry with her. She knew there was something going on between Jarrod and Justin and she was also smart enough to know it involved her. Airi would hate to think she had done something to come between the twins. They were almost inseparable and seeing them barely on speaking terms really hurt.

"It's fine, Justin. I know you are a busy man. Besides, our lunches were to get me acquainted with the company and I think I have a handle on my duties," she said. Justin smiled at her from behind his big desk. It was the type of smile that usually melted her panties and she tried to keep her dirty thoughts in check. Lately, her vibrator had been getting a workout to the fantasy of both Justin and Jarrod doing wicked things to her body. She knew she was walking a fine line, wanting them both but she couldn't help it. She guessed Ivy and her two husbands were really starting to influence her. Although, she would have never dreamt she would meet two men she would want to be with.

"Yes, you seem to be finding your way around here," Justin agreed. He cleared his throat, "Airi, I need to ask you for a favor," he almost whispered. Airi found herself sitting on the edge of her seat, as if leaning in to hear what he was going to ask.

"Sure," she offered. "Anything." God, she meant

anything too. If Justin asked her to fly to the moon with him, she would.

He smiled again and she could feel her breath hitch. She wasn't sure but she might have swooned and Airi wanted to kick herself for being such a teenager every time she was around either of the Grayson men. Lord help her if they were actually in the same room together with her. It felt as though her girl parts might just burst into flames when they were both telling her what to do in unison.

"Jarrod and I will need an assistant this week while we are in Colorado." He looked her up and down and she wanted to jump up from her seat and volunteer as tribute but then she remembered she had a one year old son. Being a mom was a lot like having a bucket of cold water thrown on you while you were peacefully dreaming; now being no exception.

"Will you go with us?" She wanted to tell him yes, she really did but she couldn't.

"I would love to," she admitted. Justin's smile nearly lit up the room. "But, I can't" she said, hating the way his smile faded as he nodded.

"I get it," he said. "It's last minute."

"Not so much that, as I have no one to take care of Milo," she said.

"Do you think your sister might keep him, if it's just for a few days?" he asked. Honestly, Ivy would jump at the chance to take care of Milo. She was always saying she wished Airi would take her and the guys up on their offer to babysit more often. Airi knew her sister would take good care of him and she hadn't had a day or night off in months. The last time she left Milo with Ivy, she had no choice. She had the flu and it wasn't safe for the baby to be around her. Her sister, Slade and Holden took him for the better part of a week so she could get better and she was so grateful to them.

"I don't know," she whispered. "I can ask her."

"Only if you want to, Airi. It would be a great help to Jarrod and me," Justin admitted.

Airi nodded, "Let me call Ivy and I'll let you know," she said. "Anything else?" she asked, standing to leave his office.

"Yes," he said. "Please don't tell Jarrod I've invited you on our trip. He's been stressed out lately and having you along might help ease some of his workload and lessen his stress, although he'd never admit it. Let this just be our little surprise."

Airi wasn't sure if surprising Jarrod was such a good idea. The last time she came back from the ladies room and "surprised" him, he confirmed he wasn't interested in her, spelling it out for her in no uncertain terms. Awkward was putting the whole situation kindly but she had done her part to work her way through. She and Jarrod had found a working rhythm that seemed to fit for them and Airi was coming to accept that no matter how hot she thought Jarrod was, he just wasn't into her and she would have to learn to accept that.

"I don't know, Justin." Airi stopped, on her way out of his office, and looked back to where he sat behind his big desk. "Jarrod doesn't seem like the kind of guy who likes surprises," she said. Justin threw back his head and laughed and Airi was sure he was the most beautiful man she had ever seen.

"You seem to know my brother well," Justin said. "He doesn't like surprises at all—fucking hates them. But, this is a good one and I'm sure he'll be able to relax a little, having you around to pick up some of the slack." Justin sent her a pleading look and it was all she could do not to melt into a puddle.

"Not many women say no to you, do they Justin?" she asked. Airi wasn't sure if she asked her question out loud until he shot her his wolfish grin and shook his head.

"No, Airi. Not many women tell me no," he agreed. She shook her head and giggled, leaving his office to make her call to Ivy. A part of her wanted to tell Justin no, just to watch him squirm but she knew given the chance, she would tell him yes. Hell, she would tell Justin and Jarrod both yes to just about anything but admitting that might just land her on the unemployment line and she had to take care of Milo.

JUSTIN

Justin paced his small office, waiting for Airi to come back in with her answer. He felt like a fucking teenager, waiting for a girl to agree to go to the school dance with him. She made him feel so alive and completely unsure of himself all at once and he had to admit it was intoxicating just being around Airi. He knew Jarrod was going to kick his ass when he found out he was the one to invite Airi to tag along. But, this might be his only chance to prove to them both that the three of them belonged together.

He and Jarrod had shared women before. Hell, Justin preferred sharing women with Jarrod but he would never tell his brother that. Most women liked the idea of having the two of them in bed, once they got past their initial shock. It just felt natural to him and Jarrod never seemed to mind. But, when he brought up the subject of them sharing Airi, Jarrod bulked. He told Justin some bullshit story about not wanting to chance sleeping with an employee and possibly pissing off HR but Justin knew better. His brother was afraid of sharing a woman they both had feelings for.

Most of the women they picked up were subs who like the idea of having twin Doms playing with them. But that was where things ended, at the BDSM club. They never took women home with them and they didn't really date. It was too messy and they didn't do messy. Jarrod and he had spent most of their late twenties and early thirties building their company and they didn't have time for relationships. It was easier to pick up women at various sex clubs and play, knowing when they were all finished, everyone would have gotten exactly what they had signed up for.

Airi was the first woman either of them had wanted to share outside of the BDSM club and that scared the shit out of Jarrod. Hell, that scared the fuck out of him too but he was willing to take a chance with Airi. The more time Justin spent with the single mother, the more he saw she was worth his time and effort. He just wished there was a way to convince Jarrod he was right because him pushing Airi away was hurting them all. If Justin could convince Jarrod to take a chance on her, they might both find the happiness that was missing from their lives.

Justin heard Airi's soft knock at his door and it felt as though his damn heart skipped a beat. "Come in," he said. Airi gently pushed his office door open and the way she looked at him, so unsure and nervous, nearly did him in. Justin was sure she was about to give him bad news when she smiled at him and nodded.

"Ivy said she and the guys would love to watch Milo

for a few days," she almost whispered. He knew he was a little overzealous but he dramatically pumped his fist in the air and cheered, causing her to giggle.

"That's great," he said, willing himself to calm down. "I'm sure having you along will be good for all of us," he said. Airi nodded and smiled. He loved the way she looked up at him through her thick lashes and he wondered what she would look like kneeling in front of him, offering to suck his cock. Justin needed to get a handle on his lust if he was going to get his shit together and meet Jarrod at the hanger on time.

"Can you be packed in the next hour?" he asked. Airi nodded. "Great," he said, pulling out his phone to text her the address where to meet. "Be at that address by noon," he said as her phone chimed.

"See you soon," she said. The breathy hitch in her voice had Justin hoping for more than he should have but he wasn't willing to give up on his sexy assistant yet. If everything worked out, Airi would be trapped between him and Jarrod, thousands of feet in the air and there would be nothing his grumpy brother could do about it. Justin was ready to give them all a push because he was ready and willing to fall for Airiana Scott.

Justin worried Jarrod would get to the plane before Airi did and that might ruin the whole plan. If he could sneak their assistant on board and not have to tell Jarrod about her being a part of their quick trip until they were at least a few thousand feet in the air, things would go a lot smoother.

He felt almost giddy when she appeared at the hanger before Jarrod and he ushered her onto the plane, under the pretense of wanting to get her settled for takeoff as soon as possible.

"I'm sorry I'm a few minutes late. I had to get Milo settled at Ivy's house and then packing took a little longer than I expected. I'm not sure I brought the right things," she admitted. Justin didn't really care what Airi wore on their trip. In fact, if he had his way, she would spend most of it naked between the two of them but he thought better than to blurt that out.

"I'm sure whatever you brought will be perfectly fine. It's business casual, really," he said.

"Could I get a water? I need to take some medicine for this headache I feel coming on. I'd like to stop it before it starts." Airi looked around the plane and all Justin could do was smile and nod at her like a complete loon. She rubbed her forehead with her hand, driving home the point she was suffering and Justin quickly found her a bottle of water.

"How about you take your medicine and then lay down for a bit? The plane has a private master bedroom," he offered. He took her bag from her and showed her back to the bedroom. Airi suspiciously eyed the big bed that took up most of the room.

"I don't know that I need to take a nap, Justin," she whispered. "It's just a little headache, probably from rushing around and worrying about Milo," she said.

"Still," Justin put her bag in the corner of the room,

not giving her any options. "You should try to relax while you can. Once we get to Colorado, we will have meeting after boring meeting," he said, crossing his eyes. Airi's giggle filled the cabin and he couldn't help his own laugh. She had a way of bringing his silly side out; the one he didn't show to many people. Justin liked who he was when he was around Airi and he hated how he allowed himself to push her away this past week. Every time he thought about picking up her favorite take out for lunch; he'd remind himself of the disastrous way their last lunch ended and changed his mind.

"Alright," she conceded. "If you don't mind me having a short rest, I'll take you up on your offer." She kicked off her high heels and Justin noticed the way her sexy little toes were painted a cute pink color. Hell, he thought just about everything Airi did was sexy but he loved the fact that she went the extra mile when it came to taking care of herself.

Airi followed his gaze down to her feet and then looked back up at him as if he were crazy. Without her heels, she was so much tinier than he was. He stood at six-three and he was pretty sure she was at least a foot shorter than him. He took a step back from her, not wanting to do what every instinct in his body was telling him to do—reach out to Airi and pull her into his body. Justin didn't trust himself to keep his hands to himself.

He cleared his throat and pasted his smile back into place. "Take all the time you need," he said. "Jarrod and I will be working while we fly, so it's not a big deal."

What he really wanted to do was offer to crawl into bed with her and hold her against his body but he was also sure that would be a bad idea. Having Airi on this trip might have seemed like a good idea earlier that morning but having her within touching distance was wearing down his defenses.

"Thanks, Justin," she said around a yawn. She rested her hand on his arm and he leaned into her touch. Airi seemed a little unsteady and Justin wrapped his arm around her.

"Woah honey, you alright?" Airi snuggled into his body and he shamelessly sniffed her head, loving how she always smelled like peaches and sunshine. When they first hired her, he would call her into his office for no other reason than when she left, his room would smell like her. Really he was pathetic when it came to anything having to do with Airi but he really didn't give a fuck.

"I'm just a little woozy," Airi whispered into his neck. He picked her up, loving the way she felt in his arms pressed up against his body and gently laid her on the bed. "I'm so sorry, Justin."

"Shh, honey," he crooned. He helped her get under the covers and made sure she was comfortable. "You just rest. Maybe we should find you a doctor," he said. Seeing her like this had Justin worried. She was usually so capable and full of energy.

"No," she insisted. "I'll be fine. I sometimes get migraines and I took my medicine. I just need to lay down for a few minutes and then I'll be as good as new," she promised.

Justin hesitated, "I don't know," he said.

"Please, Justin," she weakly begged. "I am looking forward to this trip," she whispered. He hated the way Airi looked at him, pleading with him to let her tag along. She looked so young and helpless he sometimes forgot Airi was a twenty-two year old single mother who had the entire world weighing down on her shoulders. Justin knew some of her background and he read the police reports surrounding her sketchy ex. He hated the fact that asshole ever had the chance to lay one finger on Airi or that he was Milo's father. As far as he knew though, Cole Summers wasn't a part of Airi or Milo's lives anymore and he planned on making it his business to keep Airi's ex far away from them both.

Justin nodded, "Alright, honey. You rest and if you're not feeling well by the time we land, I'll have a doctor meet us at the house." He watched as Airi snuggled under the covers and closed her eyes. He could have stood there and watched her sleep but Jarrod's arrival had him hurrying from the back bedroom.

"Hey," Jarrod dropped his bags and nodded in Justin's direction. He looked more relaxed than he had in weeks and Justin almost felt bad he was hiding a sexy little secret, who had the ability to ramp up his brother's anxiety in sixty seconds flat in the next room.

JARROD

"Hi," Justin smiled. "You ready to hit the road?" Jarrod laughed at the expression their dad used every time he dragged the two of them on one of his famous fishing trips when they were kids. Jarrod tried not to think about their dad but when his brother quoted his corny sayings, he had no choice. Their mother had left them when they were just kids and they were lucky enough to have their father. He took up the slack and became both parents for them and Jarrod was sure he and Justin were the men they were today because of their dad. They owed him everything and he was sure Justin felt the same way.

Justin's smile turned sad, "Maybe we should make some time for a quick fishing trip while we are at the house this week," he said. Jarrod nodded. Going out to their Colorado house always felt like going home. It was the house he and Justin spent the most time in with their father. It was their dad's favorite vacation spot and he ended up buying the house when the twins were teenagers, claiming they needed to spend more time outside and less time in front of the television. They both thought their father demanding to spend time with them was a punishment but now they would both give just about anything to have just ten more minutes with him.

"Yeah," Jarrod sighed. "We really should spend some time at the river. Dad would have tanned our asses for going out to the house and not picking up a fishing pole." Justin smiled at the mention of their father and fishing and Jarrod made a mental note to dig out their fishing gear while they were in Colorado. It was time for he and Justin to reconnect and there was no better place or activity to make sure that would happen.

"I'd like that," Justin agreed. "Now sit your ass down and let's get this bird in the air." Jarrod laughed at just how eager his brother was to get on their way. He had to admit he was feeling the same way. Jarrod was looking forward to putting some space between him and their sexy assistant and hopefully gaining some much needed perspective. Although, he was sure he'd need to travel a hell of a lot further than just a few states to do that.

Jarrod sat down in his seat and waved off Justin when he offered him a scotch. He was hoping to hit the ground running and alcohol wasn't going to help him do that. What he really needed was to get some shuteye but every time he closed his eyes, he saw Airiana's beautiful face, her smile and even her sexy little giggles assaulted his senses. He knew from experience alcohol only made it worse. The few times he drank while trying to forget how much he wanted Airiana, he found himself making stupid decisions like calling her at home to ask where she put a file. He was sure she thought he was crazy but at the time the lame excuses for calling made sense to him.

He reclined and by the time they were an hour into the flight, he had to admit, he was feeling pretty damn relaxed. His brother, on the other hand, seemed like a barrel of nerves and Jarrod didn't miss that Justin was on his third scotch.

"You wanna slow down, brother? I know you're not crazy about flying but you're acting strange, even for you." Jarrod shot Justin a look and his worry only seemed to intensify. "I'm starting to worry you are up to something, Justin. You have the same guilty look you used to get, when we were kids," Jarrod teased. Justin stood and paced, telling Jarrod everything he needed to know—he wasn't going to like what his brother had to say next.

"You're right—I might have done something you aren't going to like," Justin said, shooting him a sheepish grin.

"What the fuck did you do, Justin?" Jarrod growled.

The bedroom cabin door swung open, as if on cue, and Justin groaned in frustration. "Perfect timing," he moaned. Jarrod could tell his brother wasn't finding anything perfect about the timing of their sexy assistant emerging from their back bedroom.

"Fuck," Jarrod spat, sending Justin an accusing

glare. "You're right, I'm not going to fucking like what you've done," he agreed. Jarrod's relaxed, good mood quickly faded.

"Um, I can just go back in the bedroom," Airiana whispered, turning to go back but it was too late. Jarrod knew she was there. He knew his brother had taken it upon himself to push him to admit something he wasn't ready to say. Hell, he would probably never be ready to share that he was falling for their assistant. He would never be able to tell either of them she was all he could think about day and night. He'd never admit he wanted her more than he wanted his next breath because Justin felt the same way about her. He could see it in his twin brother's eyes every time he looked at Airiana and he would never do anything to hurt his brother or his chances with a woman he so obviously wanted.

"Stay," Jarrod ordered and Airiana stopped in her tracks. He felt like an ass for frightening her and the way she was watching him, he definitely had. "I'm sorry, Airiana. I don't mean to scare you. It's not you I'm upset with but my brother for making a decision without consulting me." He shot Justin another glance, letting him know they were going to have a nice long talk later when they landed and could be alone.

"I did what I had to do, Jarrod. You weren't going to listen to reason and left me no choice. All you had to do was be honest with me and Airi, and we could have avoided all of this." Justin crossed the small cabin to stand next to Airiana and Jarrod almost swallowed his tongue when she willingly let his brother pull her into his arms.

"How are you feeling, honey?" Justin whispered. Airiana leaned into Justin's body and Jarrod felt an irrational wave of jealousy. He needed to remember Airiana wasn't his and would never be. He had no claim on her and if his brother wanted to assert his hold on Airiana, he had every right.

"Much better, thank you," she said. "I'm so sorry if my being here has caused any problems," she whispered. Justin pulled her in for a hug and Jarrod had to look away. It was almost too much, watching the two of them together and not being the one touching Airiana.

"Not your fault, honey," Justin said.

"No," Jarrod agreed. "This isn't your fault, Airiana. My brother should have told me he planned on bringing a date to our business meeting. I would have made separate accommodations had I known."

"I'm not his date," Airiana stuttered. "I'm here as your assistant—both of yours," she motioned between the two of them.

"I don't need an assistant for this trip," Jarrod grumbled. He knew he sounded like a raging ass but he didn't care until he saw the hurt in Airiana's eyes. He wanted to take back his hateful tone and the way he denied he didn't need her.

"I thought we could work a few things out," Justin spat. "You don't need to be an asshole to Airi just because you were caught off guard." His brother was right, he was treating Airiana badly and that was the last thing he wanted to do.

Jarrod wanted to go to her and touch her the way she was allowing Justin to but he didn't make a move towards the two of them. He needed to remember he wasn't a part of whatever Justin and their assistant had going on. And, from the looks of it, they had something happening between them. It was what Jarrod told himself he wanted—Justin and Airiana together. Hell, he had convinced himself his twin brother would be better suited for Airiana and Milo. He'd make a better surrogate father and a hell of a better boyfriend. Jarrod wasn't boyfriend material and playing with someone as young and naive as Airiana wouldn't be fair to her or to her son. She needed stability and care and those were two things he couldn't give her. She deserved love and Jarrod wasn't the right man for the job. He wasn't a fall in love kind of guy and he never would be.

"I know exactly what you hoped to work out between the three of us, Justin," Jarrod accused. He hated the way Airiana gasped and the way she leaned into Justin's body for comfort. His brother was all too willing to wrap a protective arm around their assistant, as if she needed protecting from him.

"I'm sorry, Airiana," Jarrod said. "I thought I made myself perfectly clear last week, though." Airiana's eyes flared with anger and he was happy to see something besides hurt staring back at him. Jarrod could deal with her anger so much easier than knowing he had hurt her.

Airiana took a step towards him and God, he

wanted to take a step back but he wasn't a coward and he certainly wouldn't hide from his assistant. He meant what he said and there would be no backing down, no matter how angry Airiana looked.

"Yes Jarrod, you made yourself perfectly clear last week. You don't want me. In fact I believe your exact argument involved something to the effect of me being too young for the two of you and your worry over the fact that I could run to human resources." Airiana shook her head at him, as if disgusted by the whole memory and she took his breath away, she was so fucking beautiful.

"Yes," he agreed. He didn't miss the knowing smirk on his brother's face and he wanted to tell him to cut it the fuck out. The last thing Jarrod needed was Justin pushing Airiana in his direction because Lord help him, he'd want to catch her.

"I don't know what I have done to give you the impression I'm even interested in you, Jarrod. Either of you," she turned to face Justin. His brother's smirk quickly disappeared and was replaced with hurt. Jarrod hated to see his brother's disappointment and he wanted to stop Airiana. He wanted to tell her it was alright for her to want Justin because his brother was a great guy and deserved to find someone to make him happy. Jarrod had seen firsthand that Airiana was someone who might fit the bill for him.

"Hey, what did I do?" Justin protested.

"You stopped being my friend," Airiana accused. "You stopped showing up to my desk with lunch or to even ask how I was doing. For the last week I've

contemplated what to do about you both and my
position with your company. I don't want to stay where
I'm not wanted," she all but whispered. It gutted Jarrod
to hear her say she thought about leaving them. He
could see the disappointment on Justin's face and he
knew if they didn't get their shit together, losing Airiana
was a very real prospect.

"You can't leave us," Jarrod worried. "We need you,
Airiana."

Justin nodded his head in agreement. "He's right,
honey. I'm an ass for shutting you out like I did this past
week. I was just so confused and it seemed like the
right thing. I don't want to hurt you, Airi," Justin
admitted.

"You won't hurt me, Justin. I know my place and I
know my 'feelings' for the two of you have no room in
my position as your assistant." Airiana made air quotes
around the word "feelings" and Jarrod was pretty sure it
was one of the cutest things she had ever done.

"So, are you admitting you have feelings for us,
Airiana?" Jarrod asked. He knew better than to ask her
that question but he had to know her answer.

She seemed to take forever to make up her mind
about whether or not she was going to answer him.
Jarrod took a step towards her at the same time Justin
did. Airiana was almost sandwiched between their two
big bodies and he could feel the electricity humming
through the cabin of the plane. He wasn't a fool. Jarrod
knew there was an undeniable attraction between
Airiana and them but he also knew acting on it might
just change everything between them. He didn't want to

jeopardize his relationship with his brother if he fucked this up with Airiana and losing her was out of the question. Airiana was damn good at her job and messing things up with her wasn't an option, especially now that he knew she was considering leaving them.

"Um," she squeaked. Justin smiled and cocked an eyebrow at him, looking over Airiana's head as she fidgeted in place. Jarrod seemed to understand his brother's unspoken question and he wanted to tell him he was in. He knew that doing so would mean he'd be accepting the ways they could all be hurt when whatever this was between them ended.

"Come on, man," Justin begged. "Don't be a fucking coward. Take a chance—she's worth it." Airiana looked between the two of them, seeming confused by the one-sided conversation they were having. The two of them were always able to communicate with just a simple look and that used to drive their father crazy.

"I'm not really sure what is happening here," she whispered. "But I'd like to be clued in." She put her hands on her hips and looked every bit the part of hot, sexy mother. Justin barked out his laugh and turned Airiana to face him. He didn't give her anytime to protest or even think for that matter. His brother hauled her up against his body and sealed his mouth over hers and all Jarrod could do was stand there like a voyeur, watching the two of them, hoping like hell she'd give him a turn. Yeah, Airiana was wearing down his resistance and from the way she was letting Justin kiss her, it was only a matter of time before she found her way in between the two of them.

AIRIANA

Justin licked and nipped his way into her mouth and Airi couldn't help her breathy little moans. He tasted like heaven and a part of her knew she could easily get lost in Justin Grayson. If she was being completely honest with herself, she had already lost a piece of her heart to him after all their lunches and playful banter. He was so easy to fall for, unlike his brother. She broke their kiss and looked back to where Jarrod was watching the two of them. From the look he had on his handsome face he was turned on by the whole scene but Airi knew from experience getting him to admit to that would be damn near impossible. Jarrod had turned her away every chance he got and she was betting now would be no exception.

The two men had effectively sandwiched her body between both of theirs and she felt so slight in the middle of them. She could feel the heat pouring off their bodies and the hum of their desire filling the plane's cabin, almost as if it was tangible. Airi wanted them both but she worried if Jarrod turned her away this would all end, here and now. Justin seemed to only be on board with everything she wanted if Jarrod agreed to play. He was so quiet Airi worried Jarrod would turn her away, leaving her needy and aching for them both.

"Is this an all or nothing thing?" she whispered. "If Jarrod doesn't want me, will you still Justin?" she asked. She hated the way she almost sounded as if she was pleading with Justin to want her but she didn't care. His kiss had her body revved up and it had been a damn long time since any man touched her, let alone kiss her the way Justin just had.

"Jarrod wants you, baby. He's just over thinking this whole thing." Justin shot his brother a look and Airi could tell they were doing the silent communication thing they always did. She usually felt a little lost when they talked that way.

"Is he correct, Jarrod?" she asked. She faced him refusing to hide. Jarrod looked her up and down as if trying to decide if she was worthy and a part of her wanted to cover her body with her arms but she didn't. Airi firmly planted her feet and left her arms at her side, letting his eyes roam her body. The way he looked at her felt as though he was physically touching her and she couldn't help the small moan that escaped her lips.

"What if he is, Airiana?" Jarrod asked. God, she loved the way he used her full name. No one called her by it but him. Every time Jarrod said her name, her panties felt a little more damp from her arousal. Airi leaned into his body, wanting him to touch her the way Justin had but Jarrod had made no such move.

Finally, after what seemed like an eternity, Jarrod leaned into her body, stopping just a breath away from her lips. Justin was pushed up behind her, anchoring her between the two of them. Airi could feel her own breath hitch with need and desire. Hell, it felt as though she was panting.

"What are you waiting for?" she whispered, her lips almost touching Jarrod's.

"I'm waiting for you to come to your senses and stop me, Airiana. I'm waiting for you to tell me no." His growl told Airi everything she needed to know—Jarrod was just as much on edge as she was. He wanted her as much as she wanted them both. After weeks of denying himself from taking what she so willingly wanted to give to them, Jarrod was finally ready to accept everything from her.

"That's not going to happen," she breathed. "I will never tell you no, Jarrod, either of you," she said, reaching around her body to touch Justin. He moaned into her hair and thrusts against her ass, letting her feel every inch of his erection press against her through their clothing. Airi suddenly felt hot, as if they were all wearing too many clothes. She needed to remember getting naked with her bosses wasn't something she should be doing. There were already rumors flying around the break room at work about the three of them. People weren't blind, they could see the way she looked at both Justin and Jarrod. It was bound to be noticed at some point but she wasn't ready to announce to the world she wanted a three way with her twin bosses.

"You should, Airiana," Jarrod said. Airi was having trouble following their conversation. Her brain was muddled with lust and all she could think about was Jarrod kissing his way into her mouth and claiming every inch of her needy body.

"I should what?" she whispered. Airi gently kissed the soft skin of his neck, daring to push him, wanting more from him.

He groaned every time her lips made contact with his skin and she took it as her sign he liked what she was doing. "You really should have told me no, Airiana," he growled. Jarrod wrapped his arms around her waist and hauled her against his body. His kiss was rougher than Justin's. Jarrod seemed to want to consume her, almost as if he wanted to mark her as his. He nipped and licked his way into her mouth and she moaned at the sensations that were humming through her body as they both touched her. Their hands were everywhere and she wasn't sure where she ended or they began and she didn't care. Jarrod and Justin were giving her everything she had asked for and hopefully, they were going to give her everything she ever wanted.

"Fuck, you taste good, honey," Jarrod said, breaking their kiss. He looked over her shoulder at Justin, who was kissing and biting his way down Airi's neck. She knew she would wear his marks but she just didn't care.

"I wonder if she tastes that good everywhere," Justin moaned, biting down on her shoulder. She yelped from the bite of pain and when he ran his warm tongue over the spot, Airi was sure she would melt into a puddle.

"You like that, don't you, Airiana?" Jarrod asked. Airi nodded, not trusting her own voice. "We need to hear you, honey," Jarrod ordered. "Justin and I won't do anything with you or to you unless you give us the words." They removed their hands from her body and took a step back, effectively ending all the pleasure they were giving her. Airi groaned in frustration, instantly missing their mouths and hands on her body.

Justin chuckled and she spun around to face him. "This isn't funny, Justin," she grumbled, pointing her finger into his chest. "I'm not playing games here. If you are, then we need to stop this right here and now. It's been a damn long time since I've been with a man, let alone two. Well, that technically has never happened but you know what I mean." Airi knew she was rambling and judging from the sexy smirk Justin wore, he didn't seem to mind.

"I think we get it, baby," Justin said. "You don't want games and neither do we," he promised. "We just need to hear you say the words if you want us to proceed." Airi hated when Justin and Jarrod teamed up. It would always be two against one and she wasn't sure the odds would ever be in her favor.

Airi suddenly felt less sure of herself. She wanted them both but if things went south, and they usually did, she would be left jobless and how would she take care of her son. Everything she did in life centered around Milo and making good decisions for him. When she got out of the foster care system, she made some questionable decisions and Cole Summers was her worst. Airi ended up pregnant and had no one to turn to, so she stayed with Milo's father and let him hurt her. Every time she landed in the hospital with a new bruise and even some broken bones, the nurses would beg her to leave Cole—but she didn't. She was afraid of having to take care of her baby on her own. Leaving him, with her sister's help and support, was the best decision she ever made. Airi knew she couldn't go back to making questionable decisions just because her body hummed to life every time her two sexy as sin bosses entered the room. She knew better than that now.

"I'm afraid if I say yes you'll stop wanting me," she whispered.

"That's not possible," Justin admitted. She shot him a look of disbelief and slipped from between the two of them, instantly missing being shielded by their bodies. Before she jumped into bed with them she was going to need to make sure they both knew the score. She wasn't out for just a good time like the women who they picked up at the club. Airi needed stability in her life, someone—or in this case, two someones—who wanted to stick around and be a part of her life as well as Milo's. She wasn't looking for promises or sweeping declarations but she needed some reassurances they weren't going to dump her after they were finished using her.

Airi sunk down into one of the plush leather seats and didn't miss the looks of disappointment on either of her boss's faces. "I'm sorry guys but I can't just jump into bed with you. I have my son to think about and making hasty decisions hasn't worked out for me in the past. Milo's father was—difficult to say the least." She hated that just a few minutes ago, she was wrapped up in them, kissing them and now, she was spilling her guts about her biggest mistake.

"We know all about that asshole ex of yours, Airiana," Jarrod growled. She shouldn't have been surprised they had researched her past before hiring her on at Grayson Industries but a part of her was.

"You investigated me?" she whispered. Justin crossed the small cabin to sit down on the seat next to her, pulling her onto his lap. She should have told him to leave her alone but honestly she needed the comfort he was offering. If she was going to have to verbally relive her dark past, she might as well do it wrapped up in her sexy boss's arms. Jarrod tentatively sat next to them, seeming a little lost as to what to do or how to act around her still.

"We did, baby," Justin said. "Jarrod and I won't let just anyone into our personal lives and being our assistant, you would be privy to our daily lives and information most people don't get to see. After HR did their thing, I hired someone to dig around a little and well, look into your past." She wanted to be angry but she honestly couldn't blame them for wanting to be cautious.

"For someone so young, you have been through so much," Jarrod whispered. He pulled her hand into his own, resting it on his chest. Airi could feel Jarrod's heart beating through his dress shirt. "We won't push you Ariana but we won't hurt you either. You have to know that would be the very last thing we would intentionally do." Airi nodded, trying to decide if she wanted to ask her next question. It was easier to pretend her bosses were clueless about her past but a part of her needed to know just what she was getting into.

"How much did you learn about me?" she hesitantly asked. From the look on Justin's face, she had her answer—they knew everything.

JUSTIN

J ustin banded his arms around her middle, pulling her tighter into his body. God, the way Airi was watching the two of them nearly gutted him. He wanted to tell her that her past didn't matter to either of them but it did. After he and Jarrod got their report back from the private investigator they hired, they were dumbfounded that the same confident, capable woman who interviewed with them could go through so much shit and come out seemingly unscathed. Airiana Scott was the strongest woman he had ever met and he wasn't about to let her think her past left her wanting in some way.

"We were given a full report about your life, Airi. We learned about your parents' deaths and you and Ivy being put into the foster care system. I'm so sorry you had to go through that," Justin whispered.

Jarrod seemed just as upset about Airi's story as he felt. His brother pulled her hand to his mouth and gently kissed her knuckles. Justin loved the way Jarrod seemed to want to comfort Airi because he honestly felt the same way.

"Our mother left us when we were just six," Jarrod offered. He shrugged as if it was no big deal but Justin remembered how much their mother's leaving affected his brother. Jarrod didn't speak to anyone besides him for months. Their father dragged Jarrod from doctor to doctor trying to figure out what was wrong with him but he just needed time.

"I'm so sorry," Airi offered. "That had to be rough, on both of you."

Jarrod nodded. "It was," he whispered.

"I don't know how a parent could willingly walk away," Airi said. "Milo is my life and sure, it's hard being a single mother but I wouldn't give up a single second with him." Jarrod smiled at Airi's mention of Milo. Justin knew his brother had been sneaking up to the daycare center to check in on the little guy. He was a cute kid and easy to fall for, much like his mother.

"We at least had our father," Justin continued. "You had no one."

"Well, for a while I had my sister. We were lucky to get into a few good homes and they were able to keep us both together. But then, Ivy aged out of the system and I was left alone. They moved me a few times and Ivy lost track of me. That's when things got bad," she croaked.

Airi paused and Justin thought she was going to end her story there. He wouldn't push her, neither of them would. Telling her story was something they would let her do on her own, even if they knew how it ended—they wouldn't push.

"I was placed with an awful family and let's just say their teenage son liked me a little too much," she whispered. Airi swiped at her hot tears and the sight of her crying was too much. Jarrod seemed to feel the same way, pulling her onto his lap from Justin's and wrapping her in his arms. Justin hugged her from behind, cocooning her with their bodies.

"I'm so sorry, baby," Jarrod crooned. "You don't have to talk about it if you don't want." Airi shook her head and wiped her eyes.

"No," she insisted. "I don't talk about this to anyone —well, except Ivy and I'm careful about what I tell her. She feels so guilty about leaving me when she really had no choice." Justin watched as Jarrod held Airi, knowing whatever happened between the three of them after Airi had spilled the truth about her past, Jarrod wasn't going to just let her go.

"His name was James but everyone called him Jimmy," she started. "I was just sixteen and the family I was placed with had four other foster kids besides me and their son, Jimmy. I had to share a room with two other girls who were both younger than me but I didn't mind. Honestly, I liked sharing a room with them, it was like having a sister again and I missed Ivy." Jarrod and Justin were quiet, letting her get everything out. The thought of losing Jarrod made Justin a little crazy, he couldn't imagine what Airi must have felt or what she went through.

"At first, everything was great but then Jimmy

started coming into my room late at night and crawling into bed with me. I thought it was one of the other girls since they would both crawl into bed with me when they were scared or had a nightmare. When I realized it was Jimmy, I threatened to tell his parents and he acted as if he didn't care. He told me to go ahead and tell them because they would never believe me. I had no choice," she sobbed and buried her face in her hands.

Every protective instinct Justin had come roaring to life and he wanted to find this Jimmy and beat the shit out of him. He knew it had happened years ago but listening to Airi relive her torturous past made it feel fresh and new, as if it happened to her yesterday.

"Of course you didn't, honey," Justin offered. Jarrod shot him a look, and Justin could tell his brother was feeling the same way as he was. Jarrod wanted a few minutes alone with Jimmy to work out some of the anger and frustration they were both feeling.

"Jimmy told me if I didn't do what he wanted he would just take it from one of the two younger girls. They were just eight and six," she sobbed. "How could I let him do that to either of them? They were just babies. I was sixteen and well, I knew I could do what he wanted if it meant protecting the other girls."

"Fuck," Jarrod swore. "You were just a baby yourself, Airiana." Airi sat between them and allowed them both to wrap her in their arms. Justin wasn't sure where she began or they ended. Airi letting them hold her was everything.

"That was my first time but it didn't stop there. He kept coming back and eventually, I ended up pregnant," she whispered. "I had to tell an adult, so I told my foster mother thinking she would help me but I was wrong. She told me I was a liar and her son would never do those things to me." Airi shrugged as if it was no big deal but Justin could tell it had cost her everything. "I was moved to another home and two weeks later, I lost the baby," she cried.

"I'm so sorry, Airiana," Jarrod apologized. "It wasn't your fault—none of it was."

"I know that now," she said. "But, at the time I was a mess. No one believed me about Jimmy and when I lost the baby, I was actually relieved. What kind of monster feels relief when she miscarries her own child?" Airi sobbed and stood from her place between them. They both reluctantly released her but stood to flank her sides. Justin needed to be near Airi, even if she was refusing to let them touch her.

"You weren't a monster at all, honey," Justin soothed. "You were a scared kid who was all alone in the world. You wouldn't have been able to take care of that baby. Hell, they would have probably taken the baby away from you and placed him or her in the system. You can't beat yourself up like that." Airi laughed and Justin knew she didn't believe a word he had said.

"It's funny you choose those words, Justin. That is exactly what I did but instead of punishing myself, I let my boyfriend do that for me. When I got out of the system, I had nowhere to go. Ivy never found me and I was afraid she found out what had happened to me and didn't want me. I had run away more times than I cared to count and was labeled a problem teen." She laughed but Jarrod and he found the whole story less funny.

"What happened next?" Jarrod prompted. He knew his brother knew damn good and well what happened to Airi next, they both did. Jarrod was probably wanting her to tell him herself though, knowing she wasn't done venting.

"Next, I hooked up with my ex—Milo's father. His name is Cole Summers and he made me promises I was naive enough to believe. God, I thought I had finally found someone who cared about me but I was so wrong. After I got pregnant, he started hitting me. It got to the point where he was breaking bones he threw me around so much." Justin didn't hide the frustrated growl that escaped his chest. The thought of any man doing that to Airi made him crazy. She was so tiny that he imagined any man would cause her a great deal of damage if he laid his hands on her.

"If this is too much," she said, shooting Justin an apologetic look. The last thing he wanted her to do was apologize for anything that happened to her in her past.

"No," he said. Justin took a chance and pulled her into his body, loving the way she willingly let him. He hooked his finger under her chin, forcing her to look up at him. He needed for Airi to see he was one hundred percent on her side and the only way to do that was to look her in the eyes.

"I'm so sorry you had to go through all of that,

honey," Justin said. Jarrod pushed up behind Airi and wrapped his arms around her from behind.

"We both are," he offered.

"But not all men hurt women," Justin soothed. "Jarrod and I would never do those things to you," he promised. She gifted him with her smile, nearly taking his breath away.

"I know you are both good men and would never hurt me physically. I'm just worried about what you can do to me emotionally," she admitted. Justin loved how honest she was with them. He wanted to promise her she had nothing to worry about on that end either but he couldn't make her that oath. The storm still raging in his brother's eyes told him he might not be able to offer Airi what she needed from them and that worried him.

"We can't promise you that," Justin admitted.

"What we can promise is we would never intentionally hurt you, baby," Jarrod crooned. "How about we make you the promise if something bothers or hurts any of us, we sit down and talk it out? We've been going about this all wrong, Airiana. I'm sorry you have been caught in the middle of Justin's and my disagreement. I can't promise it won't happen again. What I can tell you is I will do everything in my power to not let our hot-headed tempers hurt you again." Airi seemed to weigh Jarrod's offer and Justin felt as though he was holding his damn breath waiting for her to answer.

After what felt like an eternity, Airi nodded. "I'd like that, Jarrod. I want to try," she whispered.

"Thank fuck, baby," Jarrod breathed.

"Be sure," Justin warned. "Once we do this Airi, you will be ours. Are you sure you want both of us—you know a package deal?" He hated asking her that. It almost sounded as if he was giving her an ultimatum but he wouldn't move forward with whatever this was that was happening between the three of them without Jarrod. As far as he was concerned, they were a package deal because he wouldn't hurt his brother just to have Airi in his bed.

She smiled up at him, "I want you both, Justin. I know this is an all or nothing deal and I wouldn't want it any other way. But, you have to know it is also the case for Milo and me. If you both don't want to deal with a one-year-old who has horrendous mood swings, isn't potty trained, only uses the word 'No' and likes to sleep in bed with me, then we can't move forward."

Jarrod chuckled, "You just described Justin," he teased. Airi giggled and Justin wasn't sure if he should laugh or deck his brother. Honestly, it was good to see them both laughing. It had been a few tense weeks between the three of them and he was just happy to know things might get better. Hell, he was hoping to get to the part where he could kiss Airi again but he wouldn't rush her. Right now, he would just take what he could get.

JARROD

J arrod was so fucking happy to see Airiana smiling and even laughing. Her story nearly broke his heart and watching her rebound and agree to be theirs so quickly only reminded him of just how strong a person she was.

"We know Milo and you are a package deal, baby," Jarrod said. "You don't know this but I sneak up to daycare to check on the little guy. Hell, I could spend most of my day in there, playing with him." Jarrod smiled just at the thought of seeing Milo sitting in the nursery, watching the older kids jumping around and playing. He loved how inquisitive Airiana's son was.

"I hate to burst your bubble dude but we know," Justin said. Airiana giggled and nodded when he sent her a questioning look.

"Yeah, the daycare likes to inform the parents if our little ones had any visitors. I actually had to approve you both being able to go into the room with him, not that most of the women up there would stop either of you." Airiana shook her head as if disgusted but her smile gave her away. "The women go on about you two every time you so much as stick your heads in to say 'hi' to Milo. I can't get any information about his day, other than the fact one of you stopped in to play trucks with him." Airiana giggled again and Jarrod couldn't help his own chuckle.

"Well, I didn't mean to cause a commotion but I do enjoy checking in on him. And well, I love when he shares his trucks," Justin shared. Jarrod found it funny that they were both not only taken with Airiana but they were smitten with her son.

"So, what's the verdict then?" Jarrod tugged Airiana's body against his, loving the way her breath hitched. "Are you going to give us a chance, Airiana?" She looked between the two of them shyly, as if pretending to size them up but Jarrod could tell from her expression she had already decided.

"Yes," she whispered. "I want to give you both a chance," she agreed. Justin took it as his green light and wrapped her in his arms, pulling her against his body for a long kiss.

"Hey," Jarrod jokingly protested. "You are hogging our girl," he teased. Airiana wrapped her arms around his neck and pulled him down, giving him every ounce of passion she had just given to Justin. She was like a drug to him and Jarrod was sure he'd never get enough of her.

"We need to go over a few rules," he said as soon as she broke the kiss. Airiana was panting with need and his cock was straining at its zipper trying to break free but his stupid brain wanted to go over a few rules? Justin and Airiana both moaned in frustration, making him smile.

He held up his hands, as if in defense. "I know guys but we have to be smart about this. We need to communicate or this won't work." Jarrod and Justin had shared women many times before but never one they wanted a relationship with. This was new territory for all three of them and he didn't want to fuck it up.

"Have you ever been in a threesome before?" Jarrod questioned Airiana. A part of him didn't want to know the answer because if she had, he would just want to rip the other two guys apart. He had never felt so possessive of anyone in his life.

"No," she quietly whispered. "You know my sister is married to Slade and Holden but I've never been in a threesome." Jarrod huffed out his breath and nodded.

"Have you two shared a woman before," she asked. Justin shot him a look that told him he should tread lightly and he had to agree.

"Yes," he answered honestly, "But not with one we wanted a relationship with," he finished.

"So, you both want to be in a relationship with me?" she asked.

"Yes," they both said in unison.

Airiana giggled, "You guys do that a lot, you know."

Justin smiled, "We know."

The captain called over the intercom to let them know they would be landing at the Denver airport in less than ten minutes. Jarrod hated that they were going to have to cut their conversation short but he was anxious to land and get Airiana back to their cabin.

"We need to get buckled in, honey," Justin said, helping her into a seat. He knelt in front of her to buckle her in and Jarrod didn't miss the flash of desire in her eyes.

"Do you like that he's buckling you into your seat?" Jarrod asked. The smile on his brother's face told him what he needed to know.

"I can tell she does, brother," Justin teased. He let his hands run up her bare leg, hitching up her dress as he went. Jarrod took the seat on one side of her as Justin took the seat on the other, putting her in the middle of them, right where they wanted her.

"She smells so good," Justin said, flashing him a wolfish grin. "She is definitely turned on by all of this." Airiana gasped at Justin's bold statement and both men laughed.

"Don't worry, baby, you'll get used to him. Justin likes to talk dirty," Jarrod said. Her blush was adorable and he wanted to see just how much further she'd let them push her.

"Let's have some fun while we land," he said. "Would you like that, Airiana?" Her blush deepened and she shyly nodded.

"Yes," she breathed. "What will you do to me?"

"Well, this is why we need rules, honey," Justin whispered into her ear as he nuzzled his way down her neck. Jarrod loved her shiver. "We like things a little rough and a whole lot dirty but only if you're up for it," he finished.

Airiana didn't answer at first and Jarrod worried with her past she wouldn't agree to everything they wanted from her. But her slight nod told him he might just get everything he had wanted for the past few months, wrapped up in one sexy as sin package.

"I want that too," she whispered against Justin's lips, just before he sealed his mouth over hers.

"Good, baby," Jarrod hissed into her ear.

AIRIANA

Airiana was having trouble concentrating with the way they were both touching and kissing her body. She knew she should be nervous about the plane landing, as she usually felt when she flew anywhere. But, the two big, sexy alpha men on either side of her were quite a distraction from her usual nerves.

Jarrod's praises seemed to warm her body from the inside out and the way Justin was kissing her, marking every inch of her skin with his mouth, she felt just about crazy with desire for them both.

Jarrod dipped his hand into her dress, finding the front latch to her bra to release it. "Tell me this is alright, Airiana," he begged. She nodded but then remembered their earlier warning of needing her words.

"Yes," she hissed as he snaked his hand in to find her taught nipple. He exposed her breasts, sucking one into his warm mouth, driving her over the edge every time his tongue softly rounded the nipple.

"You taste so fucking good, baby. I can't wait to get you to our cabin so I can taste you everywhere," Jarrod promised. She wasn't sure if she was going to be able to make it to their cabin without finding her release. They had her so worked up, all she could think about was coming.

"Please," she panted, "Please, Jarrod, I need more." She heard how needy her own voice was and she wanted to laugh, not quite sure who the woman was sitting between the two of them, begging them for everything.

"I've got you, honey," Justin said. He ran his big hand up her thigh, inching her dress up as he moved closer to her hot core. He was going to find her very wet and ready for them both. She should have been embarrassed by how wet her panties were but from the way Justin hissed out his breath when he dipped his hands into her wet folds, she could tell he liked it.

"I'm so wet," she moaned.

"Yes you are, honey," Justin agreed.

"God, I just need to taste you, baby," Jarrod's hand joined Justin's as they let their fingers play through her drenched pussy. She was so ready to come but she loved the way they were exploring her.

Jarrod and Justin both withdrew their hands at the same time, causing her to mewl her protest. She watched them as they both licked her juices from their fingers, sucking them into their mouths. Their moans and praises made her crazy with lust. She had never felt so desired or wanted in her life.

"So fucking good," Justin praised. Jarrod enthusiastically nodded his head in agreement, dipping his head in for a hard kiss. She could taste her arousal on his tongue every time he thrust it into her mouth, mimicking what he promised to do to her pussy. He reached down and pinched her nipple between two fingers causing her to gasp, first with the pain of it and then the undesirable pleasure she felt. A new surge of wetness filled her core as Justin's fingers found their way to her clit, stroking and loving it until she came, shouting out both of their names. Her cries and moans filled the cabin and she worried the captain heard her. The plane touched down and she moaned her protest.

"What's wrong, baby?" Jarrod asked. His sexy smirk was in place telling her he knew exactly what she was upset about.

"I wanted to play with both of you," she pouted.

"Well," Justin said, clearing his throat, "We have a limo and an hour's drive to do just that, honey." They both stood and pulled her back to the bathroom. "You freshen up and we'll have the luggage taken care of," Justin offered. Airiana nodded and disappeared into the bathroom.

She spent a few minutes looking at her reflection telling herself she was crazy for letting her bosses touch her the way she just did. The woman who stared back at her was almost unrecognizable. She was a wonton sex goddess who didn't give a fuck what Airi was trying to explain to her. The woman in the mirror wanted the two hot men who waited for her on the other side of the door and judging from the resolve in the woman's eyes, there would be no changing her mind. Airi shook her head and pulled back the loose blond strands of hair that had fallen around her face. When she was in public with the guys she was going to have to play the professional assistant but when they were all alone she'd happily play the wonton sex goddess for them both.

Airi hoped she hadn't just made the biggest mistake of her life but there would be no turning back now. She wanted them both and she was done with denying herself. In her short life she had learned there really isn't a promise of tomorrow, so she might as well go after what she wanted now—because that might be all she had.

———

Airi got herself together and by the time she left the bathroom, she found both of the guys waiting for her by the exit as if anxious to get on with their limo ride. She flashed them her best smile and took Jarrod's offered hand, allowing them to help her down the stairs of the private jet. She thanked the captain and was sure she blushed, worried he had overheard what the guys did to her in the cockpit before landing.

She slid into the back seat of the limo and the guys flanked her sides, not giving her any room. Airi could feel the raw desire pouring off each of them and it didn't take them long to give the driver their address and put up the privacy partition.

"Fuck, I want you, Airi," Justin admitted. "But I'm so afraid of pushing you too hard." Airi wanted to assure him she wanted them—all of them.

"You are going to have to tell us what you like and don't like us doing to you, baby," Jarrod insisted. "We expect your honesty; can you give us that?" They were both so serious she knew whatever they had planned for her it was going to be intense.

"Yes," she whispered. "You will have my communication and my honesty," she assured them. "I want you both, everything you want to give me. Please," she begged. Jarrod didn't need to be asked again, seeming to take charge of the situation, which didn't surprise her. Jarrod was usually the one in charge of things when the three of them were working. When they had their business meetings, just the three of them, Jarrod was the one to lead it and make sure everything was going according to plan. Her bosses might look identical, with their dark hair and hazel eyes but their personalities were so different.

Justin was the easier going of the two but he was still bossy and in a pinch, when Jarrod was out of town or couldn't make a meeting, he easily slipped into the role of being the one in control. Airi wondered if it would hold true in the bedroom. Jarrod, on the other hand seemed to always have everything together, although now that she knew him better, she could see the intense storms that raged on behind his beautiful hazel eyes.

"On your knees, Airiana," Jarrod ordered. She didn't hesitate, not wanting to give him any reason to believe she wasn't completely on board for whatever he and Justin wanted from her. She sank to her knees in front of him, causing both he and Justin to moan in unison. She giggled at the way they were so in sync.

"Is something funny?" Jarrod questioned, cocking his eyebrow.

"No," she sobered. "I just think it's cute the way you two are always saying the same things at the same times. You even moan at the same time." Jarrod shot Justin a look and she worried she said something wrong.

"We are not cute," Justin grouched. "There is nothing cute about either of us, honey." She smirked over to Justin and wanted to argue with him but the look on his face had her rethinking her plan.

"Maybe I chose the wrong adjective," she squeaked. "Um, how about adorable?" she asked. Both guys groaned in unison and this time she tried, really tried, to stifle her giggle.

"I think we should give her sexy lips something to do besides giggle," Jarrod growled. Airi stopped laughing as he lowered the zipper to let his cock spring free.

"Yeah, less funny now, right baby?" Jarrod asked. He watched her as if looking for any signs she wasn't fully committed to what he and Justin were asking her for. She was sure they would see no signs of regret or indecision on her part. She wanted them, both of them —all of them.

"Come here," Jarrod ordered, palming his own cock. Airi let her tongue peek out to lick him and he moaned at the sensation. "Yes," he hissed. Take all of me, Airiana," he ordered. She did just as he asked, feeling both of their eyes watching her every move. Airi reached to run her hand over Justin's erection through his pants, loving the way he thrust into her hand.

"I need her." Justin's voice sounded gruff and she wanted to go to him, give him what she was already giving to Jared but she waited to be told, knowing Jarrod would want to control every aspect of what she was doing.

"Airiana, suck Justin's cock like a good girl," Jarrod commanded. "Get him off and then I want for you to ride me, baby. Would you like that?" he questioned.

Airi nodded, "Yes Jarrod, thank you," she said, working her way to kneel in between Justin's thighs. She helped him to free his cock, not waiting for his approval. She greedily sucked Justin into her mouth and to the back of her throat, loving the way he seemed to lose control. He worked his way in and out of her mouth, using her, fucking her until he came in hot spurts down her throat.

"So fucking good, honey," Justin praised. She climbed up his body and kissed her way into his mouth. Jarrod pulled her from Justin's arms and onto his lap.

"My turn," he said, working her dress up over her head. He and Justin were watching her again, their hands were everywhere on her body and within just seconds they had her completely naked. Jarrod seated her hot core over his throbbing cock and she slowly slid down his shaft, moaning with the pleasure of having him fill her completely.

Airi wasn't sure how she was going to feel about having two men take her at once but she had to admit it was damn hot. The way Justin watched her as if he couldn't wait for his turn again, was a complete turn on. Jarrod pulled her down to crush her mouth with his own, groaning when her tongue shyly poked out to meet his. It was the hottest experience she had ever had with a man—but this time, there were two.

Airi shamelessly rode Jarrod's cock, taking what she needed from him. She could tell just by the desire on his face he was close to losing all his tightly held control. "Fuck baby, I'm not going to last," he moaned. Jarrod threw his head back and pumped into her body, as Justin pulled her over to kiss his way into her mouth. Having them both touching her and taking what they needed from her sent her over the edge as she moaned out their names, she could feel Jarrod's release as he pumped his seed deep into her core.

They cocooned her with their bodies and kissed every inch of her while whispering their sweet praises and Airi knew she had never felt so wanted, desired or God help her—loved, in her life.

JUSTIN

The whole trip had gone better than Justin had expected. A part of him was waiting for the other shoe to drop or for Airi or his brother to change their minds but they hadn't. Watching Jarrod with Airi was like watching all his dreams coming true. He had spent so much time wanting her but not knowing if Jarrod would give into his own feelings was a living agony. Finally being able to touch and kiss her was almost like living in a dream and he didn't want to wake up. The trip to the cabin took long enough to make Airi theirs—both of theirs and he knew he might never get enough of her. Justin was just hoping she and Jarrod felt the same way.

"I hate to say this, baby but we are almost to the cabin," Jarrod said. He helped her pull her dress back on and Justin wanted to protest. He wouldn't want to embarrass Airi by dragging her into the house naked. It would be the first time he and Jarrod brought anyone to the cabin. Out of all the places they owned together, their place in Colorado felt the most like home. Their father bought it when they were just kids and they spent the majority of their childhood at the cabin. It was where they both developed a love for the outdoors and bringing Airi to their place felt like a bold move. He almost didn't feel prepared for the fact she might not like their cabin and he wasn't sure why her opinion mattered so much to him.

He was starting to realize so many of his recent decisions were based on whether or not he thought Airi would approve. Justin found himself picking out shirts and ties she mentioned she liked him in, to wear to work, hoping she would notice he was wearing it. Although he'd never admit any of that to her; Airi's opinion was starting to matter to him and if he had to guess, to his brother.

Airi straightened her clothes and watched out the limo's back window as they wound down the property's long driveway. Airi had been to the penthouse apartment they shared when she first started working for them. She had delivered some contracts that needed to be signed but they really hadn't invited her in and given her the grand tour. They barely knew her then and inviting her into their home didn't feel right. Now, he was sure he not only wanted to invite her in and show her around but he wanted Airi to stay. They would get to that later though, when he was confident Airi and Jarrod were ready to listen. Right now, everything was still so new; he didn't want to rush things between the three of them and scare either of them off.

Justin was the risk taker, so unlike his brother. Jarrod was the cautious one and the most like his father. He would always look at the situation from every angle, carefully weighing and measuring the pros and cons before taking the first step. Justin was always the one who jumped from the high dive without checking to see if the pool had water in it. His father used to tell them Justin was wild just like his mother and he knew it scared Jarrod. When they were teenagers, Jarrod admitted he worried Justin would leave just like their mother had. Justin tried to reassure him he wasn't going anywhere but it never seemed to be enough. Even now, after they had built corporations together and owned houses all over the world, he could tell Jarrod was still waiting for Justin to get tired of it all and bolt. He had no way to prove to his brother he wasn't going anywhere, other than just sticking around.

"This is us," Jarrod almost whispered. Justin could tell his brother was just as on edge as he was, hoping Airi would like their place.

"Wow," she hissed. "This is beautiful," she gushed.

"Really?" Justin questioned.

"Honestly, it's fantastic," she insisted. "And is that a stream?"

"Yes," Jarrod said. "Our father used to take us fishing in it. Justin and I were thinking about doing a little fishing while we are here." Justin was happy to hear Jarrod was still willing to spend some quality time together. He felt they still needed to reconnect, especially now that Airi was in the picture. They needed to make sure they were both on the same page so they didn't fuck this whole thing up with her.

"Maybe while you two are fishing, I can do a little shopping. I'd love to get something small for Ivy for taking care of Milo. Hopefully I can find him something too." Justin smile and nodded.

"Sure honey, that sounds like a plan. You can even use the car," Justin offered.

"Let's get settled and then we need to head into the office. Work first, then more pleasure," Jarrod said, hauling Airi against his body for another quick kiss. Justin helped her out of the back of the limo and he could tell his brother was nervous about something but he just couldn't figure out what. They finally had Airi where they both wanted her but Jarrod seemed more nervous than ever.

Jarrod grabbed their bags and led the way into the cabin, "Um, how about we give you a tour and then you can freshen up," Jarrod offered. He headed down the hallway, to where most of the bedrooms were and Justin didn't miss the way he hesitated.

"You good, man?" Justin asked. Jarrod shot him a look letting him know he wasn't.

"I'm not sure what to do here, guys. This is a first for us, Airiana," Jarrod whispered. Justin knew his brother was worried about overstepping or assuming anything that might scare off Airi.

"I thought you said you shared women before," she asked. Airi looked between the two of them, almost as if she was accusing them both of being liars.

"We do—we did," Justin confirmed. "We've just

never had a woman we shared in our home before. Jarrod and I either played with subs at the club or asked women to meet us at hotels. We've never gotten to the next stage with any woman before."

"Next stage?" Airi questioned.

"Sure, the next step," Jarrod corrected. "You aren't just some woman we will use and then throw away, Airiana. Whatever this is happening between the three of us, it's more than just a quick hook-up at the club or a one night fling," he admitted. Justin wanted to agree but he was afraid their admission would have Airi running away from them. They had only just made her theirs, talking about it being more permanent or even a "thing" might have her running for the hills.

"I'm not sure I'm following," Airi admitted. "If you don't want me staying here with the two of you, I can find a local hotel." She tried to take her suitcase from Jarrod's hand and he pulled it away from her.

"I think we're fucking this all up," Jarrod growled, shooting Justin an accusatory look.

"Well, don't blame me, man. You're the one being nervous and shifty. Just tell her what you want. Tell us both what you want, man." Justin ran his hands through his unruly hair and let out a frustrated growl. He was sick of trying to figure out what his brother was feeling or what he wanted. It was time for Jarrod to make some sweeping declarations so he knew they were on the same page. Taking Airi was a no brainer but Justin was starting to worry making her theirs for the long run was going to be a challenge.

"I'm sick of trying to guess what you are feeling, Jarrod. Tell her—tell us," Justin ordered.

"He's right," Airi's soft voice agreed. "I've admitted I want you, Jarrod. I want you both. What do you want?" she questioned. "I told you I don't want to play. If you've changed your mind, just say so and I'll find another place to stay."

"No," Jarrod barked. "I haven't changed my mind. In fact, I'm trying to figure out how to convince you to stay, here—in my room. But that would be selfish of me, because what about Justin?" Jarrod looked between the two of them and Justin almost wanted to laugh at just how pained he seemed.

"Why can't you just share me, like you did on the plane and in the car?" Airi questioned, smiling up at them. Her question was so earnest Justin couldn't help his own smile.

"Well, I don't see why we can't," Justin said.

"That means we pick a bedroom and all bunk up together?" Jarrod's question caused Airi to giggle and Justin had to admit, his brother's expression cracked him up.

"Yes," she simply said.

"Yep," Justin agreed.

"Alright then," Jarrod turned and led the way to one of the master bedrooms he used whenever they were in town. Justin wasn't about to argue about which room they were using; he really didn't give a fuck which bed they slept in as long as Airi was cuddled in between the two of them. Things were progressing so quickly; Justin knew Jarrod was having trouble keeping up with the changes. It was just who his brother was—a worrier, an over thinker. He was also someone who once he knew what he wanted; he went after it. Justin was just happy his brother was finally going after Airi because not wanting her wasn't an option for him.

JARROD

After they unpacked and freshened up, the three of them headed to their Colorado headquarters. The office was in a frantic uproar over a merger that wasn't going according to plan. If the deal fell through, Greyson Industries stood to lose millions. It wouldn't be the first time a deal went south and costed the company a good deal of money but it had been a damn long time since it happened. He and Justin had taken extra measures to hire a good team of people to help build their company. They also took cautious risks that made them money without causing them too much trouble.

They spent most of the afternoon putting out small fires and working with the Colorado team to make sure things started running more smoothly. Having Airiana there made the unbearable situation more pleasant. The problem was he spent most of the afternoon hard and counting down the minutes until he could strip her bare and sink back into her body. He knew Justin was just as on edge but his brother tried to hide his desire for Airiana. Jarrod knew she would want to keep things professional while at the office, and he had to admit he felt the same way. The last thing any of them wanted or needed were the office gossips spreading the word the three of them had fallen into bed together. And if he knew Justin, he knew his brother wouldn't want to deal with HR getting involved in their private lives.

Jarrod was hoping after their last meeting, Airiana would let them take her to their favorite steak house for dinner and then back to their house to spend the night between the two of them. While they were sitting in the meeting, Airiana's phone chimed and she sent them both an apologetic glance. But the way she turned the ghostly shade and quickly stood to exit the meeting; Jarrod was ready to throw his desire for privacy out the window and chase after her. Justin's subtle shake of his head had him double thinking whether he should follow Airiana out of the conference room but God, he wanted to. The meeting dragged on for fifteen more agonizing minutes until they decided to call it a night and pick up everything in the morning.

"What was that?" Jarrod spat, trying to calmly leave the room when all he wanted to do was run out of there to find Airiana.

"I have no idea but let's go find our girl and we'll figure it all out, together," Justin offered.

They found Airi sitting in the office they both shared when they were on site, sobbing into her hands. Seeing her so upset did crazy things to his heart. Every protective instinct in him screamed at him to go to her and comfort her. God, he would do just about anything to fix whatever was causing her to be so upset. But he wasn't the one to scoop her up from her chair and cradle her limp body against his own—that was Justin. His brother was the one whispering to Airiana everything was going to be alright while kissing her face. A pang of jealousy ran through Jarrod and he knew he needed to squash it but he wasn't sure if he'd be able to. He hadn't felt that way watching his brother take Airiana or make her his own. It turned him on to watch them together but watching his brother take care of Airiana and sooth her, somehow had his green-eyed monster roaring to life.

He needed to shake it off and get his head back in the game. His jealousy wasn't fair to either Airiana or Justin. "What happened, baby?" Jarrod asked.

"Ivy texted that Cole was trying to see Milo," she sobbed into Justin's suit jacket and Jarrod couldn't take any more. He crossed the room to where his brother held Airiana and pulled her from his brother's arms into his own.

"Cole, as in Milo's father, right?" Justin asked as Jarrod took his turn to soothe their girl.

"Yes," she stuttered. "He's never really taken an interest in our son."

"Has he had any visitations with Milo?" he asked.

"No, he's never met Milo," she said. "Why would he all the sudden want to see him?" Jarrod wished he had an answer for her but he didn't.

"How would he know to contact Ivy?" Jarrod questioned.

Airiana sniffled and Justin handed her his hankie. Jarrod sat on the leather sectional in the corner of their office and put Airiana on the sofa between the two of them. He knew Justin would want to touch her and comfort her as much as he did.

"It's a long story. When Ivy found me, I was still with Cole. Slade had a little heart to heart with my ex and explained to him my baby and I would be better off without him," she whispered.

"Remind me to take Slade out for a beer when we get back to town," Justin drawled. Jarrod smiled and nodded. He had to agree with his brother. Knowing Slade stood up for Airiana when no one else was around to made him a good guy in his opinion.

"Ivy and the guys took me in after Cole told me he didn't want anything to do with me or Milo and that was the last time I had heard from him," she said. "How would he get Ivy's information?" she asked.

"I'm not sure, honey but we'll look into it. I hope you'll let us help you?" Jarrod watched her, as if worried their wanting to help her and Milo might seem a little over the top. He wouldn't hide the fact he and Justin would want to take care of her but he knew Airiana was an independent woman who was used to handling being a single mother. He wondered just how much she'd allow them to help her.

"You would want to help us?" she questioned. Justin chuckled and pulled her against his body.

"Of course, honey," he agreed. "We want to help you in any way we can."

Jarrod wrapped his arms around her body, gently

kissing her lips. "Say you'll let Justin and I help you, Airiana," Jarrod asked.

She nodded against him, "Yes," she conceded. "Thank you," she whispered.

"You never have to thank us for something like that, honey," Justin said.

Jarrod had a nagging feeling they were missing something. Why would her ex wait until she was out of town to try to get to Milo? Was he watching her and waiting for the right time to strike? That thought had him so mad he felt about ready to punch someone. Justin seemed to notice his shift in moods and sent him a questioning look. Jarrod shook his head not wanting to get into everything and upset Airiana further.

"Did he show up at Ivy's house wanting to see Milo?" Jarrod asked. He knew the more information he had to pass onto his head of security, the easier it would be for them to find this Cole Summers and have a chat with him. This time, he and Justin would let Airiana's ex know if he came around again there would be hell to pay.

"No," she said. "He dropped by the bar, where my apartment is," she said.

"You live above a bar?" Jarrod questioned.

"Yes," she answered sounding somewhat defensive. "Didn't your little search on me mention that?" Jarrod let Justin handle the search and his twin hadn't mentioned that Airiana and Milo live above a bar.

Jarrod tossed Justin a sideways glance and his brother had the nerve to shrug. "I didn't think it was pertinent information," Justin said. "So, I left off the

little bit about the two of them living over Cash's bar
—Manholes."

"Perfect," Jarrod groaned. "You and Milo live above
a gay bar." He wasn't sure if he wanted to laugh or be
furious about the whole mess. He knew he was being a
possessive asshole and that might just scare away the
first woman he wanted a relationship with but he didn't
care.

"Let's not put the cart before the horse, brother.
Once step at a time," Justin said, as if able to read
Jarrod's mind. "What happened when he showed up to
the bar?" Justin questioned.

"Well, Cash called Slade over from the club and
Cole seemed to remember Slade from the first
conversation they had. Apparently he made quite the
impression," she giggled. It was good to hear her laugh.
Jarrod worried Airiana would be consumed with fear
over Cole wanting to get to her son but their girl was so
resilient.

"I'm sure he did, baby," Jarrod smiled. Slade Kelly
would protect anyone he thought of as family with his
own life. Jarrod had no question Slade would protect
Airiana, since she was Ivy's little sister.

"He told Cole to leave me and Milo alone but Cole
didn't listen to reason this time. He told Slade he'd be
back and warned that Slade couldn't protect me
twenty-four hours a day," she sobbed. Jarrod hated they
had circled back to her crying again.

"No, Slade can't do that, honey. But, we can," Justin
said. "There is no fucking way you are going back to
your apartment to wait for Cole to show up again. We

all know he will and I won't put you or Milo in danger."
Jarrod had to admit he was happy to hear his brother
say that but he worried it would scare off Airiana.

"I have nowhere else to go," Airiana said. "Ivy and
the guys are going to have a baby and the last thing
they need is Milo and I taking over their home. I have a
perfectly nice apartment and a good lock on my front
door. Cole won't do anything stupid and if he does, I'll
just call the police."

"Did that work for you the last time?" Jarrod asked.
He knew he sounded like a complete ass but he didn't
care. If they couldn't convince Airiana to let them
protect her and Milo, she'd be a sitting duck once they
got home.

"No," she spat. "It didn't. But I'm older and wiser
now. I won't let Cole hurt me again and there is no way
I would ever let him hurt my baby," Airiana insisted.
"How could you think that of me, Jarrod?" God, he
hated she believed he could so easily hurt her. That
would be the very last thing he would ever want to do.

"I know that, baby but you might not have a choice
in the matter. I'm assuming he's bigger than you? What
if he overpowers you and hurts Milo or worse, takes
him?" The sob that escaped Airiana's chest nearly
gutted him. Jarrod seemed to be fucking the whole
thing up and saying all the wrong words.

"I'm sorry, honey," Justin soothed. "My brother is
being an ass." Justin shot him an accusatory look,
telling him to let him handle things. But Jarrod didn't
want to sit back and let his brother clean up his fucking
mess.

"He's right, baby and I am sorry. You have to remember this is all new for both of us. We've never been in a relationship with a woman we shared. We are trying to figure this all out as we go and I'm afraid I'm making a mess of everything." Jarrod tried to leave the sofa but Airiana stopped him, pulling his arm back to make him stay.

"No," she whispered. "Please don't," she begged. "I'm the one who should be sorry. You were just trying to help. You both were and I was just lashing out. I'm worried he will find a way to make good on his threats and that thought scares the hell out of me. I can't lose my son—Milo is my whole world." Airiana covered her face with her hands again, letting the sobs rack her body. Jarrod pulled her small, shaking body into his own, not quite knowing what to say next. The three of them sat like that for what felt like an eternity until he finally knew what to do.

"Move in with us," he whispered.

"What?" she asked. He wasn't sure if she heard him or if she was questioning his sanity at asking her to move in with he and Justin after only being together for less than a day.

"He asked you to move in with us, honey," Justin offered. "You and Milo could move into our place. We have plenty of room and you would be safe with us."

Jarrod loved how his brother was on board with his crazy plan. He had just made a huge decision that would effectively change Justin's life but he took it all in stride, even seeming to like the whole idea.

"We couldn't," Airiana gasped.

"Sure you could," Jarrod countered. He knew their conversation could go around in circles all night and get them nowhere. "How about we do a trial run? You and Milo move in with us and if it doesn't work out, Justin and I will help you find someplace safe to live. Just until your ex can be stopped." He sounded like he was begging but he didn't give a fuck. Jarrod needed her and Milo safe and if he had to beg to do it, he would.

"Fine," she finally agreed.

Jarrod wasn't sure what he and Justin had just gotten themselves into but a part of him felt as though they had just won the lottery and their pretty assistant was their prize.

AIRIANA

Airi wasn't sure if it was the right time to tell them she had convinced her brother-in-law, Holden Kade, to bring Milo to Colorado or not. She planned on telling them as soon as they got back to the cabin but she wasn't sure the guys would be very happy about having to share her time with her son. She had played the conversation over in her head, during their short trip from the office to the cabin, but she was being a coward. There was no way she'd leave Milo anywhere near Cole. Holden worked for Grayson Industries and he was going to have to make the trip to Colorado in a few days, anyway. She was just asking him to fly out a little early and bring her baby with him. She completely trusted Ivy and the guys to keep her son safe. Still, she wanted him near, just in case, and now Airi was being a chicken about telling the guys about their soon to be tiny visitor.

"Um," she squeaked. Airi realized her son and Holden would be in Colorado the next day and not telling them might cost her their trust. "I have a little confession to make." Jarrod and Justin both stopped what they were doing to give her their full attention and she almost wished that wasn't the case.

"You can tell us anything, baby," Jarrod prompted, wrapping his arms around her body. She was starting to get used to them touching her and calling her little pet names but every time they did, her heart still raced like a teenage girl's. She wondered if she would ever get enough of either of them.

"Baby, I can see the hesitation on your face; you need to just tell us," Jarrod insisted.

"You're starting to worry us, Airi," Justin agreed.

Airi sighed against Jarrod, knowing they were right, she just needed to tell them. "Milo is on his way here," she all but whispered. "Holden is bringing him out tomorrow when he comes for his meetings. Please don't be angry with me," she begged. The last thing she wanted was for either of them to be angry for going behind their backs to make arrangements with her sister and Holden to get Milo to Colorado. As soon as Ivy texted her telling her about Cole showing up at Manholes, she ran out of the conference room to call her sister. When she realized her son was in danger, she asked to talk to Holden. She knew Milo was one lucky kid to have an aunt and uncles who loved him so much but Airi wanted him close. Holden agreed to travel to Colorado with Milo in tow, since he already had business to attend there. Her only other option would have been to cut her trip short with Jarrod and Justin, to head back to her son and that was something she wasn't ready to do.

Airi wanted to soak up every minute with the guys. A part of her was worried that as soon as they all got back to town, the fantasy world they had been living in would disappear and she would go back to her lonely nights of wanting them both but not having either of them. Now that they had asked her to move in with them, a part of her was hopeful it wouldn't be the case. She worried they were rushing things, moving her and Milo into their place but she had to admit she was grateful. She knew raising Milo over a bar wasn't a good plan but she was grateful for a place to live and at the time, it was all she could afford. Maybe she'd be able to save up some money living with the guys and if things didn't work out she'd be able to get a place of her own. Either way, she was thankful she wouldn't have to face the new threat of her ex snooping around, causing trouble, alone.

"Airiana," Jarrod said. "Why didn't you tell us sooner?"

"I arranged everything while you finished your meeting. I wasn't sure how you would react, so I didn't tell you at first. But, I'm telling you now," she whispered.

Justin crossed the bedroom to sit next to her on the end of the bed and took her hand into his. She loved the way they were constantly touching her, seeming to crave the same connection she needed. "Well, I think it's a great idea, honey," Justin said. "What time will Holden and Milo get here?"

"Tomorrow evening," she said. Airi looked over to where Jarrod was watching her and she worried he wouldn't be as accepting of her son joining them.

"Again, if this isn't what you signed up for Jarrod, just say the word and I'll find us another place to stay. Heck, I'd even understand if you'd like to rescind your invitation for Milo and me to move in with you." She hated thinking about finally having everything she wanted and dreamed of for so long, only to have it all taken away from her.

Jarrod sat on the bed next to her, putting her in the middle of the two of them, the bed dipping with his weight. It felt so right to be between them, as if she was made to fit there. Her heart felt as though it might just beat out of her chest but she couldn't let it stop her from being brave enough to face Jarrod down. She knew he might tell her he had changed his mind but she wouldn't take the coward's way out and not face him full on while he told her.

"I haven't changed my mind," Jarrod growled. "I don't think I ever will, if we're being honest here, baby."

Airi nodded, "Yes, please," she whispered. "I only want your honesty, Jarrod." She could deal with just about anything, as long as she knew exactly where they stood.

"Okay well, if I'm being honest Airiana, I've wanted you for months now." She didn't hide her surprise at his admission.

"But in the office last week, you said you didn't want me. I know I changed your mind on the plane but all this time?" Airi questioned.

"Yeah," he admitted. "All this time. Hell, since the first time we met, really." Jarrod shot Justin a look and she knew they were doing the whole silent communication thing they did. "I have a feeling my brother felt the same way, baby."

Airi looked over to Justin and could see Jarrod was right. She could always tell what Justin was thinking, just from his expressions. Every time he brought her lunch or took her out for a quick bite, she could see on Justin's face it meant something to him. He'd never admit it at the time and she would never push for fear of scaring him off or worse, having him flat out deny his feelings for her. It was easier to pretend she had feelings for either of them and a whole lot less messy to deal with a platonic relationship at work.

"I do," Justin said. "I feel the same way as Jarrod. I'm pretty sure you knew that though, honey. Hell, I spent all of my free time at work trying to find some lame excuse to see you or spend some time with you."

"I kind of figured, Justin," she teased. Her relationship with him was so different than her relationship with Jarrod. Up until the last twenty-four hours, she was sure Jarrod didn't want anything to do with her outside of work.

"I know I said I didn't want you but I was being a fucking coward," Jarrod admitted. "I wanted you so fucking much but I could see that Justin felt the same way and I worried about hurting him. I never let myself imagine you would want both of us this way. I'm so sorry I hurt you, Airiana. I hurt both of you by denying my own feelings and I could have fucked up everything." Airi wrapped her arms around Jarrod's neck, needing to touch him.

"Oh, Jarrod," she whispered. "So, you're okay with Milo coming?" His chuckle told her all she needed.

"Yep," he admitted. "In fact I'm happy Justin and I will get to spend some time with him. The daycare workers don't seem to trust me with Milo. They watch me like a hawk every time I go up there."

Airi giggled, "Well, they are the best and they are just doing their job to protect my little boy," she said.

"I'm happy he's going to be here," Justin agreed. "It will give us both time to get to know Milo before he's just thrown into our crazy lives. I know moving in with us isn't going to be easy for either of you, Airi. But, I hope you give Jarrod and me a chance."

Airi worried once they got to spend a full day with her son, they might change their minds about having the two of them move into their place. She was going to have to resign herself to being alright with living each day one at a time. Airi would drive herself crazy if she tried to figure out what was happening between the three of them. One day at a time would be easier to figure out and so much tidier than jumping in with both feet.

JUSTIN

Justin and Jarrod spent most of the next day in meetings trying to put out fires, while Airi multitasked getting ready for Milo and helping the them both at work. He could see she was frazzled but he knew better than to try to stop her from doing everything. He knew his girl enough to know when she was worried about something, she tried to take on the world. Justin just wished she would let them help her more but getting her to agree to be theirs and even move in with them, was a huge step for her and an even bigger one for his brother. Although, Jarrod was taking everything in stride and even seemed excited about Milo's visit.

They spent the night wrapped up in Airi's body, and when they finally fell into bed, they slept tangled up together. Justin worried it wouldn't work; they wouldn't like spending so much time with each other but he was wrong. Airi seemed to be the perfect middle, the buffer they both needed between the two of them. It was as if she was made to fit between them and the thought of someone trying to hurt her or Milo drove him crazy. He woke up that morning knowing he was going to have to do some more snooping. Justin could tell his and Jarrod's initial background check on Airi pissed her off but he had no choice now. He needed all the information he could dig up on Cole Summers and if Airi got upset with him for snooping, he could live with that.

Jarrod attended their first morning meeting so Justin could steal away to contact their security team back home. He wanted to get the team started researching Airi's ex. There would be no way he or Jarrod would take Airi and Milo back home knowing Cole Summers was a threat. He was hoping to find the guy and have his team take care of him before they returned home. They would have a little conversation with him and if he wouldn't listen to reason, they would have to come up with plan B.

"Hey," Jarrod whispered, sneaking into their office. "Is Airiana here?"

"No," Justin said. "She ran back home to sign for the delivery of stuff I ordered for Milo. He's going to need a crib and a few other things while he's here," Justin said, smiling at the thought of all the cute boy toys he purchased. He knew Milo wasn't his but he was a pretty damn amazing kid.

"I'm excited about him coming here too," Jarrod admitted. "Did you find out anything about her ex?"

"Not yet," Justin said. "Airi's going to be pissed when

she finds out we hired another investigator to look into her ex."

"I don't give a fuck," Jarrod admitted. "My only care is keeping her and Milo safe. If that asshole wants to be back in her life, he's going to have to go through me to do it."

"Me too," Justin agreed. "There is no way I'm going to let that trash anywhere near her or Milo." He knew they had no real claim to their assistant or her son but he didn't give a fuck. He wanted Airi and as far as he was concerned, she was his—his and Jarrod's.

"You sure about all of this?" Justin asked. "I know you were worried about hurting me, going after Airi and taking what you wanted from her but that won't happen. We want the same thing here, man." Justin hoped his brother understood he meant every word. As far as he was concerned, sharing Airi was the best idea they had ever had.

"I'm sure. I denied myself Airiana for too long. I won't do that to her or you anymore. I want this and I'm sure." Jarrod promised. "We just need a damn good plan to keep her and Milo safe because I won't lose her now." Justin had to agree with his brother. The thought of anyone getting close enough to hurt their girl or Milo made him half crazy.

"I've scheduled a meeting with Holden after he and Milo get here, out at the cabin. I figured we could get the scoop on what happened back at home and Airi can get Milo settled." Jarrod agreed and Justin was happy they were on the same page. Now, they just needed to make sure Airi understood she wasn't going anywhere without either of them.

————

Justin hated the worry he saw on Airi's face while her brother-in-law recounted Cole Summers's visit to the bar. Holden had showed up at the cabin with little Milo just after they got back from the office. Apparently, the asshole had the nerve to storm into Manholes, the bar where Ivy worked and Airi lived in her tiny apartment and demanded to see his son. Cole hadn't asked to see Milo since Airi left him when she was about seven months pregnant. He had no interest in her or his son, so the question remained—why now?

"Let me get this straight; Airiana's ex just showed up at the bar and he demanded to see his kid?" Jarrod questioned.

Holden sighed and nodded. "Yes," he confirmed. "Thank God Ivy had the night off since she was home with Milo. Cash called me to let me know about him showing up at Manholes but when things got out of hand and Cash had to call the police in, Cole left before the cops showed up. They went by his place but according to his landlord Cole hasn't been living in his apartment for months. No one knows where he is and when he'll just show up again is anyone's guess."

The sob that escaped Airi's chest nearly undid him. Justin pulled her onto his lap and Jarrod took Milo from her arms. "No, honey don't cry. He's not worth it," Justin soothed, stroking his hand down her back.

Holden eyed the three of them suspiciously and cleared his throat. "Ivy insisted I tell you that you and Milo will be moving in with us, once your business out here is finished. Also, since no one has any idea where this asshole is, I suggest you both increase your security around this place, just in case." Holden said.

"It's already done," Jarrod said. Justin could tell his brother was ready to tell Holden they had the situation in hand but he worried Jarrod wouldn't be quite so congenial.

Justin spoke up before Jarrod's temper got the better of him. "We hired on extra security, just to be on the safe side this morning. We've also convinced Airi to move in with us once we are finished here. We have plenty of room for her and Milo and well, she has agreed." Justin watched Holden, waiting for him to give any argument but judging from the silly grin on his face, he wasn't about to give one.

"Yes, I can see things have changed," he teased, looking to where Justin held Airi on his lap.

"What's happening between Airi and us isn't your business, Holden," Jarrod said. Justin was sure Jarrod was overreacting but he would never tell his brother to back down when it came to his protective tendencies towards Airi and Milo.

Holden held up his hands as if in defense. "I didn't mean anything by my observation, Jarrod. We are friends here and Airi is my sister-in-law. Milo is my nephew and I would never want to hurt either of them. But, they are my business since they're both my family.

If Airi tells me they are moving in with you, then I whole heartedly approve it."

"Thank you, Holden," Airi whispered. "But I want to move in with them."

Holden smiled and nodded, "Well then, I'm happy for both you and Milo, Airi. Please let us know what we can do to help with your move."

"That's already been taken care of," Jarrod said. Justin groaned, knowing Jarrod admitting they already sent a crew over to move Airi and Milo's sparse belongings to their place was probably going to piss her off. The last thing Airi needed was to feel bulldozed over by the two of them.

"What did you do?" she asked, standing from Justin's lap. He didn't try to hold her back, there would be no use and his brother didn't have the good sense to even look apologetic.

"You agreed," he defended. Justin stood and took Milo from Jarrod. The last thing he wanted was for Airi and Jarrod to have a heated discussion with the poor little guy between them.

"Yes, I agreed to move in with the two of you but that doesn't give you the right to send strangers into my home to pack up my stuff and lug it over to your place. You can't just take over my life and make all the decisions for me, Jarrod. This relationship won't work if you keep doing that," she whispered.

Jarrod smiled at her and Airi looked at him as though he had lost his mind. Justin couldn't help his own smile. She had finally admitted what was happening between the three of them was a relationship, Airi just didn't realize it.

"Why the hell are you smiling, Jarrod? I'm yelling at you," she growled. Her frustration didn't help the situation. He and Jarrod seemed to find everything about Airi adorable, even her anger.

"Yes honey, you are. But you also said this thing happening between the three of us is a relationship," Jarrod said.

Airi seemed to go over her words, and Justin could tell the moment she realized what she had said. "Well, crap," she whispered.

"I think I'll give you guys some time to talk. I'm heading into town to my hotel. Call me if you need me, Airi," Holden said. He kissed her cheek and Milo's forehead and was gone.

"No more hiding, baby," Jarrod ordered. "We're going to talk this over and finally hash everything out. Ready or not."

Airi nodded and took Milo from Justin. "Let me put the baby down and then we can talk," she grumbled. Justin wanted to chuckle at her disgruntled tone but he knew better. He was just hoping she was ready to come clean and tell them both she was falling for them because he could see it in her eyes every time she looked at either of them. Justin was sure they were going to have their work cut out for them with their girl.

JARROD

Jarrod paced their bedroom while he and Justin were waiting for Airiana to put Milo to bed. He knew she was hiding out in the nursery they had put together that afternoon but he'd let her have her time.

"This is a relationship, right?" Justin questioned. Jarrod hated how his brother still worried he wasn't one hundred percent on board when it came to what was happening between them and Airiana. Jarrod wanted everything with her. Sure, he dragged his feet and was basically tricked by his brother to admit he had feelings for Airiana. But, once he set his mind to taking her and making Airiana his, there was no turning back for him.

"Yes," Jarrod breathed. "I want this thing happening between the three of us to be a relationship. I'm falling for her, man," he admitted. It was the first time Jarrod had let himself become emotionally involved with a woman they shared and it scared the hell out of him.

"Thank fuck," Justin growled. "I'm already in love

with her but I was afraid to admit it," he said. Jarrod could tell his brother was in deep with Airiana. He was the one who let himself become invested in their new assistant. Justin had already shared dates with her, lunches and even some dinners. He was the one building a relationship with her these past few months and Jarrod was just happy he could join in.

"So what do we do now?" Justin asked, running his hands through his unruly hair.

"I'm not sure. This is uncharted territory for the both of us. Do we tell her we are falling in love with her?" Jarrod's question was almost a whisper but he still didn't hear Airiana enter the room.

"Yes, you should tell her," she whispered back. "I'm pretty sure she feels the same way about the both of you." Airiana stood in the doorway to their bedroom and the look on her face told them everything they were hoping to hear from her. She was in love with them and Jarrod couldn't stop himself from going to her. He needed to touch her, hold her and God—he wanted to taste her.

"Say it again," Jarrod whispered, pulling her into his arms.

"I'm in love with you, Jarrod," she admitted. Airiana looked up at him and he could see her honesty shining back at him. She looked over to Justin and held out her hand, waiting for him to take her silent offer. His brother seemed to hesitate, and for a moment, Jarrod wasn't sure what Justin was thinking. Justin's easy smile crossed his face and he took her hand, pulling Airiana from Jarrod's arms into his own. Jarrod watched as his brother kissed his way into their girl's mouth and he was sure that watching the two of them together was the hottest thing he had ever seen.

"I love you too, Airi," Justin admitted between kisses.

"We both do," Jarrod agreed, pulling her between the two of them. She stood sandwiched between them, her arms around their waists, and Jarrod realized she was truly the glue that held them both together. He had come to think of her in that way at work as their assistant. But now, she was taking on that role in their everyday lives and he loved the way she seemed to fit so perfectly between them.

"So now what?" she questioned. "How do we move forward with all of my past baggage dragging me down and you two having to worry about what sharing your assistant will look like at work?"

"Fuck work," Justin said. "I don't give a shit what people think about the three of us together. HR can handle it and if anyone has a problem with Jarrod and I being with you, they can look for another job." Jarrod nodded his head, fully agreeing with his brother.

"But, it's not that easy," Airiana whispered. "You have a corporation to run and whether or not you like it, public opinion does matter. You two are in the spotlight and sharing me won't be good for either of your images." Jarrod hated how Airiana seemed so worried about their public personas but it was a part of her job. He knew she had a point but he didn't really care. They both wanted Airiana and no one else's opinion would stop either of them from having her.

"How about you let us worry about the company and what people think," Justin offered. Airiana hesitated and finally gave a curt nod. Jarrod was sure their girl would give them grief about it later but for now she was willing to concede.

"And as for your past baggage, we are working on that," Jarrod admitted. He was sure she wasn't going to like hearing that they were taking over that part of her life too but he really didn't care. Jarrod was sick of not taking what he wanted. He wanted Airiana and anyone trying to hurt her would have to answer to him and Justin.

"You two can't just swoop in and fix all of my past mistakes," she whispered. "I made them and I should be the one to fix them."

"That's not how this is going to work, honey," Justin said.

"My brother is correct," Jarrod agreed. "You need to think of the four of us as a team now, Airiana." She looked up at him and he could see the confusion on her face.

"Four?" she questioned.

Jarrod smiled, "Yep, four. You, Justin, me and Milo." Airiana's smile lit up the room at his inclusion of her son.

"Thank you for that, Jarrod," she said. "I love how the two of you accept Milo. I know this must be hard for the both of you. I'm a single mother with a crazy ex and a whole lot of baggage weighing me down but you both seem to take it all in stride."

"It's simple, Airiana. We want you and Milo to be ours," Justin said. "We love you."

"Thank you," she whispered.

"You never have to thank us for that, baby." Jarrod pulled her up his body, sealing his mouth over hers, loving the way her breathy moans filled their room as he and Justin worked to get her naked.

Jarrod was completely fine with the fact that the talking portion of their evening was over but Airiana seemed to have other ideas. She pulled her long blond hair free from the messy bun she had it tied back in to let it spill over her shoulders and he just about swallowed his damn tongue.

"We need to talk," she whispered, causing both Justin and him to groan in frustration. They had her completely naked and judging from her wet panties they had just pulled off her, she wanted them every bit as much as they did her. Justin's eyes were wild with lust and he was sure he looked about the same.

"We can talk later," Jarrod offered, a step towards Airiana. She held up her hands, effectively stopping him.

"No, I think this needs to be said now," she all but whispered. "I think you both are holding back with me and I don't like it."

Justin cleared his throat, shoving his hands into his pockets. Jarrod knew it was to keep from touching Ariana but he wasn't so willing to comply, as his brother was. God, he wanted her and not touching her was driving him crazy with lust.

"What do you mean, Airi?" Justin questioned. From

the smug smirk on his brother's face, he knew exactly what Airiana was talking about. Jarrod was pretty sure he knew too but he didn't want to waste time playing games.

"Well," she stuttered. "I've heard you two like to play at the same club Ivy goes to." Jarrod hated how uncomfortable Airiana seemed to be, talking about the lifestyle they both enjoyed. He hoped sooner or later they would convince Airiana to go to the BDSM club with them but he wouldn't push her.

"Yes, we did go to Pandora's Box, to play, honey. If you're worried about us continuing to go there, don't. We meant what we just said—we want you, Airi," Justin admitted. She seemed to deflate some and Jarrod thought she had the answer she was looking for. Airiana smiled and sunk to her knees in front of them. Jarrod hissed out his breath at the idea of Airiana being everything they needed, giving them everything they wanted. She was already the perfect woman for the two of them; her kneeling in submission almost seemed too much.

"What are you doing, baby?" Jarrod questioned. He already knew but he wanted to be sure. Hell, he wanted her to be sure but that would be asking her to re-evaluate her current position and she was gorgeous kneeling for them.

"I know that you two are Doms," she panted. "I want to be what you need," she whispered.

"You are exactly what we need and want, honey," Justin said. Jarrod could tell his brother was just as effected by their beautiful girl kneeling in front of them but he wasn't making any move towards her. It was almost as if they were both afraid to touch her, like she'd break if they did.

"I want you both, all of you. You have been holding back with me, not giving me your full dominance and I hate that. I need you to show me what you want from me. I need to be everything for you both—please," her voice cracked and her begging nearly gutted him but Jarrod knew she wouldn't take less from either of them. She wanted them—all of them and Jarrod was ready to unleash his inner caveman and show Airiana just what she was getting herself in to.

"Be sure, Airiana," Jarrod warned. He loved the way her eyes flared with desire when he growled his order at her. He already knew she was submissive but seeing her kneeling, hearing the way she so earnestly asked them for what she needed, it was almost too good to be true.

"I'm sure Jarrod, please," she begged.

"Well then, we will need some ground rules," Justin said. He pulled off his shirt and Airiana's eyes followed his bare torso, taking in every inch of him. Jarrod couldn't help himself; he did the same, loving the way she gave him the same response. Other women they played with always seemed to favor one or the other of them but not Airiana. She treated them both so differently but gifted them equally with her love and attention.

"You will need a safe word, since this is all so new for you. We will need to get to know your likes and dislikes, so a safe word is in order," Jarrod said. "Make it a word you wouldn't normally use in a conversation or during sex." Airiana squinched up her face as if trying to think of the perfect word, and he was sure it was the cutest thing he had ever seen.

Finally, she looked to the bed behind where he and Justin stood and smiled. "Bunny," she said triumphantly. Jarrod turned around to find Milo's favorite stuffed bunny, laying on the bed behind him and laughed.

"Bunny it is, baby," he agreed. "If things get to be too much for you or you just don't want to do something we ask of you, just say the word 'bunny' and it all stops." Airiana nodded her head, letting Jarrod know she was on the same page. He just hoped he wasn't rushing everything with her. Justin and he had discussed leading her into their lifestyle choices slowly. They should have known their girl was a jump into the deep end feet first kind of person. She wouldn't let them gently lead her anywhere, it wasn't who she was.

"We'll also need to go over things you like and don't like. Is there anything you'd particularly want to try?" Justin asked. They waited her out and Jarrod once again felt as though he was holding his damn breath. He worried about Airiana's troubled past with abusive ex-boyfriends and her trouble with her foster brother, she wouldn't be into shows of dominance involving force or spankings and he would be fine with that. Jarrod wanted to be whatever Airiana needed from him and they could figure the rest out as they went.

"I like it when you both tell me what to do," Airiana whispered. "I also think I'd like to be tied up—you know handcuffs, rope—all that stuff." Justin moaned and ran his fingers through her hair, forcing her to look up at him.

"What else?" Justin asked. His voice sounded gruff with need and Jarrod could tell his twin was completely on edge. Listening to her tell them exactly what she wanted was torture but it needed to be done.

"Um, I'd like for you both to be inside of me. You know—at once." Now it was Jarrod's turn to groan at the thought of how fucking good it would feel to both take her at once.

"We'll have to train your ass for that, honey. You sure you are ready for all of this?" Justin questioned. Airiana closed her eyes and nodded. "Words, Airi. We need the words or this all stops now," Justin warned.

"Yes," she hissed. Jarrod could tell she was turned on just from talking about all the dirty things she wanted them to do to her. "I want you to train my ass, Justin," she moaned.

"How about spanking, baby?" Jarrod almost hated asking, knowing exactly how Cole Summers treated her and what he did to her. But he wanted Airiana to know what he and Justin would do with her would be so much different. Spanking her ass would be solely for her pleasure, never anything as dark and disgusting as what her ex did to her.

She hesitated and Jarrod wanted to take his question back. "You don't have to answer that," he whispered. "I'm sorry Airiana."

"No," she protested. "I'm not a child and I know the difference between spanking for pleasure and the abuse my asshole ex forced me to endure. I think I'd like that, Jarrod. I just don't know. I'd like to try," she said, gifting him with her shy smile.

Jarrod nodded, "We'll take it slow, baby. Justin and I won't push and you have your safe word." His whole body seemed to hum to life when she once again nodded and he hoped like hell they were to the part where they could talk less and touch more.

"Thank you," Airiana whispered. Justin seemed to be just as impatient as he was feeling. His brother shucked out of his pants letting his cock spring free and Airiana reached for him, forgetting they were calling the shots.

"Not yet, honey," Justin said. All this talking has me worked up and if I let you touch me now; I won't last long." Jarrod smiled at his brother, as if able to read his mind. They wanted to drive their girl half-crazy with lust before she even got her hands around their cocks. By the time they finished with her, she'd be begging to touch them.

Airiana's pout was downright adorable. "We'll get to that part, baby," Jarrod promised. First we are going to see how you do with us tying you up. Would you like that?" he asked. Jarrod was hoping like hell she'd agree to being tied to their bed.

"Yes," she breathed. "I think I would like for you and Justin to tie me up, please." That was all the invitation Jarrod needed. He nodded to Justin and his brother pulled the cuffs from the bedside table.

"They are fur lined, so they won't pinch as much," Justin said, turning them over in his hands, letting

Airiana inspect them. "But don't pull too hard on them, honey. They will leave marks if you pull tight enough." Airiana nodded.

"Got it," she whispered. "Don't fight the restraints or they will pinch." Her tone was light and teasing and Justin seemed to like her playfulness. Jarrod was just hoping they weren't making a mistake, rushing her into sharing their dominance with her.

"We'll just see how much sass you have left after we have you fully restrained on our bed. I'm going to eat your pussy until you can't do anything but pull against the restraints, begging for more," Justin said. He swatted her ass, making her yelp as he passed by her to secure the handcuffs to the bed.

"Up you go," Jarrod said, helping Airiana onto the four poster bed. She smiled and thanked him as he secured her wrists to the top posts. His brother tightened the restraints around her ankles, effectively spreading her wide leaving her ready for them to do whatever they wanted.

"Fuck, you look good enough to eat, baby," Jarrod growled. "You eat her pussy, Justin while I get our girl ready." Airiana moaned and writhed against her restraints and Jarrod had to admit he liked the way she reacted to just his commands.

"I'm going to be the one giving the orders tonight," Jarrod confirmed. "But you will obey Justin too. Do you understand Airiana?" he questioned. He liked to be in control but he also liked when their subs obeyed them both. Jarrod knew Justin craved her submission as much as he did but he always yielded to Jarrod's whims and desires.

"I understand," she whispered. "Please, Jarrod. Just tell me what to do—what you want," Airiana's pleading was nearly his undoing. Watching Justin work his way down her body was enough to make him want to come in his pants. He needed to have Airiana wrap her sassy mouth around his cock and get him off if he was going to remember his need for control.

Jarrod quickly undressed loving the way Airiana watched him as he stroked his aching cock in his hands. She licked her lips, giving him all the invitation he needed to take what he wanted from her. She moaned as Justin lapped at her pussy, giving her what she needed, leaving Jarrod free to take his pleasure from her.

"Open for me, baby," Jarrod commanded. Airiana did as he asked without hesitation, beautifully submitting to him and he was sure he would never get enough of her. "So fucking beautiful," he praised as she sucked him into her mouth, playfully swirling her tongue around his shaft. He just about lost it when she sucked him to the back of her throat, taking nearly all of him. She was giving him everything the he needed and he knew he wouldn't last long.

"I'm going to come." His voice sounded horse with need. Airiana sucked him in and out of her mouth, setting a punishing rhythm and it was all he could take. He shot his seed down her throat in hot spurts and she took all of him and even protested when he pulled free from her greedy mouth.

"I need to taste her," Jarrod said. He quickly took Justin's place between her thighs and licked his way into her drenched folds. Airiana came for him, shouting out his name as she writhed against his face, shamelessly taking her pleasure from him.

Jarrod looked up to find Justin lapping at her nipples and he could tell his brother was ready to take Airiana. "Fuck our girl, Justin," Jarrod commanded. He liked that his brother let him call the shots but he could also read Justin better than anyone else. He knew how badly Justin needed to take Airiana.

"You don't have to tell me twice," Justin said. He quickly released Airiana's bindings and handcuffs and Jarrod wanted to laugh. His brother preferred women to be free to touch him and he could tell Justin wanted that from Airiana.

"Feel me, Airi," Justin ordered. She shyly smiled up at him and wrapped her hands around his cock, doing exactly as he ordered. Jarrod watched as his brother hissed out his breath and knew it wouldn't take much for Justin to lose it. Jarrod sat on the edge of the bed, watching them together and he had to admit it was damn hot. Justin licked and kissed his way into Airiana's mouth and Jarrod's cock was already hard again just from her breathy moans and sighs.

Justin pulled her legs around his cock and thrust deep inside of her, causing her to groan out her pleasure. He set a punishing pace and Jarrod couldn't take it anymore, palming his own throbbing shaft. His need for Airiana was out of control; he'd never get enough of their sexy assistant. He wanted inside of her;

needing to be where Justin was. The thought of them both being able to take her at the same time had him spilling his seed into his hand. He breathlessly watched as Justin lost himself in Airiana and they collapsed onto the bed together. Jarrod was pretty sure he had never felt more content with anyone else, outside of Justin. It was as if Airiana completed them both—she was made for them.

AIRIANA

Airiana woke to Milo's chattering over the baby monitor the guys had installed, and she couldn't help her giggle. She was surrounded by her two sexy men and wondered if last night had just been a beautiful dream. Waking up between the two of them brought home the realization she was not imagining her sexy bosses making her theirs all night long.

She decided to try to slip from the bed and go to Milo before he became too insistent and woke the guys. It was no easy feat to pull herself free from their big bodies but she finally slipped from the bed just as Milo started to fuss. Airiana pulled one of the guy's shirts on from the night before, finding her way down the hallway to Milo's nursery and when she opened the door, he squealed.

"Hi baby," she whispered. "Did you sleep well?" Airiana scooped up her son and cuddled him, loving the way he snuggled into her. Her favorite time with him was always early mornings while they were both waking up. Milo was always so snuggly and like her, a happy morning person. Airi's sister Ivy was always grumpy and she wondered which of her own parents she took after.

They died when she was so young, she couldn't really remember small character traits such as if they were morning people or night owls. It made her sad not knowing little things about her parents most kids knew and took for granted. Most days, she didn't let not having them in her life bother her but since having Milo she thought about them more and more. Airi wondered what kind of grandparents they would be and if they would want to have big family gatherings for Sunday dinners or holidays. She never had any of those things—well, none she could remember. Airi wanted all of that for Milo and she just hoped like hell she'd be around to give him everything she always dreamed of having.

After Cole kicked her to the curb, pregnant, with nowhere to go, she worried she would never be able to give her baby anything. Once Holden helped her get her job with Grayson Industries, she allowed herself to start hoping again. Airi wanted to be able to buy a house for Milo to grow up in. Something with a big back yard and maybe get a puppy. She wanted the fantasy that she never had, for her son and that was why she worked so hard. She spent every waking free minute with Milo but when she had to work, she loved knowing he was well cared for in the daycare at her office.

That was what made being with her bosses so scary for her. If things went south and Justin and Jarrod decided they were tired of playing with her, where would she go? Up until this job, her work experience had been babysitting as a teen and waitressing. She never dreamed of being anyone's personal assistant, let alone one to two of the most powerful businessmen in town. If she ended up unemployed, Airi didn't know where she would land. Not many businesses wanted to hire a twenty-two year old single mother with little to no job skills.

Airi changed Milo's diaper and spent a few minutes playing with him. She loved this age; he was so inquisitive and the wonder on his little face made her happy. He was such a happy baby and she would often just sit and watch him, trying to figure out how she had gotten so lucky in the kid department.

"Hey," Justin whispered. He entered the nursery holding a bottle for Milo and Airi thought it was the sweetest gesture.

"Sorry if we woke you," Airi took the bottle and handed it to her eager son. He loved his morning bottle almost as much as she loved her coffee.

"You didn't," Jarrod said. He walked into the nursery holding a mug of coffee and handed it to her. He reached for Milo and Airi was surprised her son went to him. She had forgotten that her son already knew both of her bosses due to their secret visits to the nursery at work.

Airi sipped her coffee and moaned at just how good it tasted. "Is it the way you like it, baby?" Jarrod asked.

"Yes," she said. "Thank you." Jarrod sat on the sofa with Milo while he drank his bottle and she and Justin joined them. The whole scene felt so domestic, so normal she almost let herself forget this wasn't her life.

"You seem a little out of sorts today," Jarrod said, studying her. The last thing she wanted was for them to see her self-doubt creeping in. She would need to deal with that on her own, not wanting to weigh either of them down with her issues. Honestly, she was already starting to feel like a burden to them, with all her baggage and past demons rising to the surface. She wished she could say that wasn't how her life usually went but she would be lying to them both. Her life had always been unpredictable and even a bit chaotic. Airi just hated how Justin and Jarrod were now caught up in her mess.

"I guess I'm just tired," she whispered.

Justin pulled her onto his lap and banded his arms around her body. "Liar," he accused. She hated that Justin could tell when she wasn't being completely honest. They had spent so much time together since she was hired on; she sometimes forgot just how well he seemed to know her.

"Is he right, Airiana? Are you not telling us something?" Jarrod questioned. She couldn't look either of them in the eyes and continue being less than truthful with them.

"Yes," she admitted. "I wasn't lying though. I am tired," she stalled taking another long drink of her coffee.

"But you're not being one hundred percent truthful

with us," Justin added. "You aren't telling us something."

Airi sighed. "I was just thinking about what will happen if things don't work out between us," she admitted. Saying it out loud made her feel as foolish as she sounded. Here they had only just begun and she was already worried about their end. That was just how her brain worked though.

"We don't even get a chance?" Jarrod asked. She could tell he was teasing from his tone but she saw the hurt in his eyes. Justin's expression was identical to his brother's and she knew that she was going to have to do some explaining.

"I've spent my entire life waiting for the other shoe to drop," she said. "When I was a kid, my parents died. I don't really remember them. Ivy and I were moved from foster home to foster home whenever things didn't work out or they ran out of room or time for us. It was inevitable, the changes in my life. I guess expecting the worst to happen is just my way of protecting myself. I plan for the absolute worst case scenario and then when bad thigs happen, I adapt and adjust accordingly."

Justin and Jarrod watched her as if they were dumfounded about what to say next. She knew her doom and gloom stance was unhealthy. Really it must have sounded downright dark as she explained everything to them but it was honestly how she was feeling, and they asked for her honesty.

"Well, that's a shitty way to have to live, honey," Justin grumbled. "How about you let Jarrod and I worry about what happens next and you just concentrate on being happy?"

She almost wanted to laugh at the idea of just being happy. Sure, she had people and things in her life that made her everyday life happy. But, it didn't change the fact she was always holding her breath, waiting for the bad stuff in life to catch up to her.

"Sure," she offered. Jarrod laughed, causing Milo to jump. Her son smiled up at him and he laughed even harder.

"You need to be more like Milo, baby," Jarrod offered. Her son looked between the three of them, grinning like a loon at all the attention they were giving him and she couldn't help her giggle.

"If only life was that easy," she said. "I'm just glad Milo is happy and doesn't have to worry about all of the bad stuff yet."

"How about you let Jarrod and I show you just how easy it can be to have some fun? We have one short meeting this morning and then the whole day is yours," Justin said. "Let us plan a fun day for the four of us?" He waited her out but Airi could tell he wanted her to agree. Truthfully, a day of fun, just the four of them sounded like a dream.

"Alright," she agreed. The guys all but cheered at her agreement, causing her to giggle again. She just hoped she didn't disappoint them. Days of fun weren't exactly her strong suit but she was willing to give it a shot if it would mean making her guys happy.

———

Airiana stayed back at the cabin with Milo while the guys headed into town to attend their meeting. They assured her Holden could hold down the fort while they took the rest of the day off but she worried she was costing them precious time at the office. Them wanting to show her a good time was great but not at the cost of the company. She needed to remember they were business owners and their trip to Colorado was purely work related, although they had slipped in a good deal of pleasure.

When the guys got home around noon, she had lunch waiting for them. Their housekeeper had left menus from the guys favorite places to eat and she ordered them some food and had it ready for them after they changed. She had to admit she liked seeing them in their gym clothes. Airi usually saw the two of them in their business attire but even dressed down, they took her breath away.

"So, what's on the docket for our day of fun?" she asked. The guys looked at each other and their mischievous grins should have told her whatever they had planned, she wasn't going to be a fan.

"First, we thought we could go for a little hike," Jarrod offered. Airi opened her mouth to protest she couldn't go hiking with a baby but Justin squashed her argument, telling her he'd purchased a toddler backpack and would carry Milo on his back. Airi really wanted to make an "Aww" sound but decided against it. Her guys weren't fans of her finding them cute. Sexy as sin, sure—cute, not so much.

"So, hiking and then what?" Airi asked. She knew

they weren't going to let her off so easily, with just a little hike. They had to have more planned and she was right.

"Well, after we go hiking, we thought we'd teach you and Milo how to fish," Jarrod said. She rolled her eyes. Airi was beginning to think their ideas of what a fun day was didn't really match up.

"Fine," she groaned. "I accept your challenge but just so you know, I see what you're up to." She knew her tone sounded accusatory but she didn't care. The guys were showing her their idea of fun, hoping it might rub off on her. She never really was an outdoor kind of girl and this little test would prove just that. She was being weighed and measured and she loved a good challenge.

Jarrod and Justin both laughed and finished their lunches while she packed a day pack for Milo. She wasn't sure either of the guys realized just what went into leaving the house with a baby in tow but they were about to get a crash course.

JUSTIN

Justin loved the feel of Milo's tiny body pressed up against his and the way the toddler chattered on in baby gibberish in his ear as he hiked up the mountain with him on his back. "If he gets to be too much, I can carry him for a bit," Airi offered.

"Nope," Justin said. "He's just fine. Besides, he and I are in the middle of a very important conversation."

Airi giggled, "Oh, I see. And, what are the two of you discussing?" she asked.

"Well, Milo would like to know if he could have some ice cream after dinner and I told him I would discuss it with you," Justin offered, causing Airi to giggle again.

"I'm all for ice cream, if we are taking a vote," Jarrod chimed in. Airi looked between the two of them, understanding just how things usually worked out when he and his brother agreed on things.

"I'm going to always be out voted, aren't I?" she asked.

"Yep," they said in unison. Airi's giggle floated on the breeze around him and Justin was sure he had never heard anything so magical. He could get used to more days like this and listening to their girl giggle because of something one of them said.

"Especially when it comes to ice cream," Justin added.

"I guess we are having ice cream," she mumbled, causing both Jarrod and him to laugh. Justin like the way it felt like they were a family unit when it was just the four of them. He hoped he wasn't the only one feeling that way, although he was sure Jarrod was getting those same vibes.

They hiked most of the afternoon and tried to teach Airi to fish, although their girl drew the line at baiting her own hook. She quickly caught her first fish and when they told her she had to clean and cook it for dinner, she threw it back into the river. Justin was sure Airi wasn't cut out for the country life but he really didn't care. Spending the day with her, Jarrod and Milo felt right.

They got cleaned up and headed into town for dinner and ice cream. Dining with a toddler was a whole new experience. Justin was sure he was wearing most of Milo's dinner and at least half of his own. They called it a night early enough to get Milo home for a bath and then bed.

Airi looked about ready to collapse and he convinced Jarrod to help him with Milo, so Airi could soak in a bubble bath. The look of horror on Jarrod's face was almost comical. Neither of them knew anything about giving a toddler a bath but it was time they learned. Milo and Airi were both moving in with them and this was going to be their new normal.

Milo splashed in the tub, trying to catch the bubbles that floated around him, while Justin and Jarrod leaned over the ledge to watch him. "Do you think Airiana had fun today?" Jarrod quietly asked.

Justin didn't have to even think about his answer. "Yes," he said. "I think even though our girl is only twenty-two, she has done a lot more living than either of us, man."

"I agree. But she's one of the strongest damn women I know and a hell of a mom," Jarrod said. "So, what do we do about her ex?"

Jarrod's question was one Justin had spent the better part of the day thinking about. And honestly, he really didn't have any answers. "We make sure he doesn't get anywhere near Milo or Airi," Justin offered.

"Agreed," Jarrod said.

They got Milo into his pajamas and gave him a bottle. The two sat on the sofa reading him bedtime stories and snuggling until the toddler fell asleep on Jarrod's chest. Justin was surprised how it all felt so normal—the way Milo fit with them. He never thought about having kids before but Milo made him want things that once seemed impossible.

"Well, there my three guys are," Airi whispered from the doorway. Justin's heart did a little flip flop at her calling them her guys. She was wearing a little nighty that barely covered her sexy curves and all he could think about was touching and licking his way up her body. Judging from Jarrod's predatory look, he felt the same way. Jarrod stood and gently laid Milo in his crib. The three of them stood over him, watching and holding their breath, praying he didn't wake up. The toddler stirred and then snuggled into his blanket, sucking his thumb to lull himself back to sleep. Justin was sure it was the single cutest thing he'd ever seen.

"That was a close one," Airi teasingly whispered. She took them both by the hand and led them from the nursery and back down the hall to the room they all shared.

"How about you read me a bedtime story and put me to bed?" she teased. Justin had to admit he liked when Airi was playful, it turned him on. His brother looked more amused than turned on but that changed as soon as Airi lost the lacy lingerie she was wearing, letting it slide down her body to the floor. She stood between the two of them completely naked and Jarrod's smirk turned into a smoldering gaze, telling Justin his brother was already in Dom mode.

"Fuck," Jarrod swore. "Every time I see you, Airiana, you take my breath away." Airi smiled at Jarrod's praise and Justin had to agree with his brother. She was breathtakingly beautiful. Her long blond hair spilled over her shoulder and the way she watched them—her blue eyes were full of mischief and promise of what she was so willing to give to them both. Justin knew they were both goners and he wouldn't have it any other way.

Justin wasn't sure if she would so happily accept what he was going to say next but he had to try. "We want to plug your ass, Airi. Jarrod and I want to take you at the same time but we will need to train your ass to take us both." Airi scrunched up her nose, her smile still in place.

"How do you feel about that, Airiana?" Jarrod questioned.

"Um," she nervously whispered. "I'm not sure how I feel about it. I think I'll like it but I won't know until I try. I've never done anything like that before. Heck, I've never been with two men at once, so this is all new to me." Jarrod's eyes flared with need at Airi's admission and Justin had to admit, he was feeling the same way. The idea of being the first men to take her ass was hot as fuck and he couldn't wait until they could make her theirs completely. First, they were going to need to take their time and work her towards their final goal. Otherwise, they would end up hurting her and that was the last thing either of them wanted. If they did this right, Airi would come to love anal and that would be win-win for all three of them.

"I'd like to try," she whispered. Justin and his brother both seemed at a loss for words but it was time for one of them to take control of things.

"How about if I take lead on this, brother?" Justin asked, looking over to where Jarrod intensely watched their girl.

"Please," Jarrod agreed, clearing his throat. "Would you like to have Justin calling the shots this time, Airiana?" he asked. She shyly nodded and it was all

Justin needed. He crossed the room to the nightstand and pulled out a black felt bag from the top drawer. He slid the three silver egg- shaped objects from the bag and turned them over in his hand, as if letting Airi inspect them.

"Wow," she said. "That one is really big. Will it fit inside of me?" He chuckled at her question and she placed the metal plug back in his hand.

"It will fit, Airi. But tonight, we will start with the smallest one," he offered. She took it in her hand and turned it over.

"Yes," she agreed. "This one is much smaller. I think I can do this," she conceded. "It's really pretty. I like the blue jewel in the end," she said, giggling to herself. "Pun intended."

Jarrod laughed at her joke and took the plug from her. "It matches your eyes, baby," he said. Justin watched as Jarrod kissed his way into Airi's mouth. He loved to watch them together; seeing Airi submit so freely always turned him on.

Justin kissed and nipped his way down her back. He knew Jarrod would keep their girl busy to the point of distraction, so he could get her ass ready for the plug. Justin grabbed the lube and worked it into Airi's tight opening, loving her breathy little sighs and moans as he plunged his finger in and out of her virgin ass. He couldn't wait to take her there, knowing they would be the first to give her that, turned him completely inside out. Airi was going to feel so fucking good too; she was tight and it was hard to concentrate on the task at hand.

Airi pushed her ass back against Justin's hand, as if

silently asking for more and he was happy to oblige. He slowly worked the smallest plug into her opening, loving the way she continued to push back against it, as if knowing what to do.

"That's it, baby," Jarrod's praise sounded like a hiss. "Just relax and let Justin work the plug into your sexy ass."

"Please," Airi whimpered. "I need more, Jarrod." Justin looked around Airi's body to see that his brother was ready to give her what she was asking for. The pleading look Jarrod shot him made him want to laugh. Jarrod was completely on edge with his own need for her. But Justin was in the same boat, and his cock being so hard it was throbbing in his pants, was no laughing matter.

"Fuck our girl, man," Justin offered. He knew Jarrod was waiting for him to give the order, having gifted him with their control over Airi for the night. He knew Jarrod needed the control and giving it up, even for a short time, was a big step for his brother.

"On it," Jarrod confirmed. He quickly stripped and sat on the edge of the bed, pulling Airi's willing body to straddle his lap, letting his cock slide into her body. They both moaned and Justin wished he was the one taking Airi while her ass was plugged.

"She's so fucking tight, man," Jarrod said. "I'm not going to last."

"Good," Justin said. "I need her when you're done." Airi moaned and threw her head back, shamelessly riding his cock, taking what she needed from him.

"You like that Justin is going to fuck your tight little

pussy when I'm done with you, don't you?" Jarrod asked.

"Yes," Airi moaned. "I like the way you use my body. Both of you," She reached for Justin and he took her hand, needing the connection. He framed her back with his body, loving the way she leaned back on him. Justin ran his hands down her sexy curves, giving each of her breasts attention. Watching the plug peeking out at him as she rode Jarrod's cock was hot as hell. Justin like seeing his handy work.

"I like this," he teased, running his fingers down the seam of her ass, giving the jeweled plug a turn. Airi seemed to like the extra attention he was giving to her ass, crying out in pleasure as she found her release. Jarrod quickly followed her over and Justin ruthlessly pulled her from his brother's cock, not giving her time to recover from her orgasm. Justin pushed her against the mattress, slamming into her body from behind.

"Fuck yeah," he groaned, setting a punishing rhythm. Justin knew he was being an ass; he just didn't care. He needed everything she was willing to give him, her body and her love. He needed her and not taking Airi wasn't an option. Justin thrust balls deep into her, loving the sound of their flesh slapping together and lost himself into her body, shouting out her name.

He pulled from her body and wrapped his arms around her. "Sorry, honey," he breathed. "I didn't mean to be so rough," he whispered.

Airi turned to face him, wrapping her arms around his neck. "I loved it," she said. "I love you, both." She wrapped her other arm around Jarrod and pulled him into their embrace and Justin knew his world was finally whole.

———

The three of them had fallen asleep tangled up in each other and Justin loved the way Airi fit between he and Jarrod. He woke to someone banging on their door and groggily looked at the alarm clock. "Who the fuck is breaking down our door?" Justin grouched.

"Whoever it is will wake Milo," Airi said.

"Fuck," Jarrod swore. He stood and pulled on a pair of sweatpants and stormed out of the room. Justin did the same and was just behind him, shouting at Airi to check on Milo.

The banging continued and Justin was sure his brother was going to rip whoever was on the other side of the door completely apart, once he got it open.

"What the fuck do you want?" Jarrod grumbled, pulling the front door open.

"Sorry guys," Holden grumbled. He held up his hands as if in surrender and looked just as tired as Justin felt.

"You know it's two fucking thirty in the morning, right Kade?" Jarrod barked.

"I know and I already said I was sorry but I need to talk to Airi." He strode past the two of them, and Justin had to hand it to the guy, he showed no fear of Jarrod's out of control temper or Justin's mean mugging him.

Airi rounded the corner and plowed right into the back of Justin and he turned to find she was wearing just his shirt. He tried to cover her with his body as Jarrod mumbled something about her needing more fucking clothes on. She swatted at the two of them and went to Holden.

"Guys, he's effectively my brother and eww," she whispered. "You're just lucky you didn't wake up my son, Holden."

"Gee, thanks for that, Airi," Holden teased. "And, sorry but this couldn't wait."

"Well, I had to say it or my protective cavemen were going to make me put on more clothes and judging from the worry on your face, I don't have time to get dressed. What's wrong?" Airi asked. Justin pulled her back into his body. If she wasn't going to put on more clothes, at least she would be in his arms and not Holden's.

"There is no easy way to tell you this, Airi," Holden said, running his hands through his hair. Justin swore he could feel Airi's heart beating.

"How about you just spill it then and we'll take it from there?" Justin asked.

"Cole Summers is dead," Holden whispered. "Ivy just called to tell me; Milo's father is gone."

JARROD

"Oh my God," Airi sobbed, raising her shaking hand to her mouth, trying to muffle the sound.

Jarrod felt about ready to lose his shit. Holden showing up to tell them about Cole Summers's death really threw them all for a loop. He hated how he felt relieved the guy was dead but he was and judging by Justin's expression, he was too. The only person who seemed visibly upset by the news was Airiana and she had every right to be. Summers might have been an asshole but she shared part of her life with him and even created Milo with the guy.

"How did it happen?" Airiana whispered. Justin sat down next to her and pulled her onto his lap, giving her his comfort. A part of Jarrod wished Airiana would turn to him and let him comfort her but she hadn't. He worried Airiana would never turn to him the way she did Justin and that realization hurt, even though he knew he was being overly dramatic.

"The police said he was murdered, shot in the chest," Holden said. "He was at his apartment and there were no witnesses. According to Summers's latest girlfriend, she found him when she returned home from her shift and nothing was missing from their apartment. They believe whoever killed him wanted him dead. It looks to have been premeditated, according to the detective Slade spoke to. Someone wanted Cole Summers dead."

"Who would want to do that?" Airiana questioned.

"No clue, Airi," Holden admitted. "But they hauled Slade in for questioning." Jarrod could tell Holden was worried about his family and he couldn't blame him. If it was Justin or Airiana being questioned in a murder case, he'd just about lose it.

"Why are they questioning Slade?" Justin questioned. "What interest would he have in Summers being dead?"

Holden shrugged, "It's no secret around town, Slade all but ran Cole off when we found Airi. He has an alibi, so he should be fine. They will want to talk to you too, Airi," Holden all but whispered.

"Me, why me? I've been here the whole time," Airiana said. Jarrod paced the floor, knowing if he sat down he'd go half crazy. His poor girl had been through enough and he wished he could spare her any more heartache.

"You and Cole share a son," Holden offered. "I'm sure it's just a formality." Airiana nodded and leaned her head back onto Justin's shoulder.

"We will all fly home in the morning," Jarrod

decided. "Holden, you need to be with your family and we need to get this mess taken care of. I'll have our lawyers head over to meet Slade at the station. He shouldn't answer their questions without representation." Holden nodded his thanks and stood to leave.

"Guys, we have to consider the possibility whoever murdered Cole might come after Airi and Milo," Holden said. Airiana gasped and the little sob that escaped her made Jarrod want to comfort her but she was still turning to Justin for that.

"We can't just take Airi and Milo back home not knowing if they are in danger," Justin said. "I won't allow it, Jarrod." Justin knew his brother was just as upset about the whole turn of events as he was but hearing him all but accuse Jarrod of marching Airiana and Milo into danger pissed him off. He would never do anything to hurt either of them. They were just as much his as they were Justin's. It was time Jarrod reminded them all of that fact.

"I fucking love them too," Jarrod growled. "You can't sit there with our girl and say I would ever put either of them in danger, Justin. They are just as much mine as they are yours." Jarrod hated that he had to say those words out loud. He thought they were past all of this but he was to blame for the jealousy he was feeling every time he saw Airiana turn to Justin for comfort instead of him. It hurt but that was on him. He was the one who let those feelings get in the way of him and what he wanted—namely Airiana and a life with her and Milo. He knew Justin wanted the same thing.

Airiana stood and crossed the room, wrapping her arms around his neck to pull him down for a kiss. She didn't seem to care that her brother-in-law sat front row center for her display. She kissed Jarrod as if she was starving for his taste and couldn't get enough of him.

"It's about fucking time," she whispered against his lips.

"You want to run that by me again, baby?" Jarrod asked.

"All this time, you've been keeping me at a distance and it's about damn time you let me completely in, Jarrod. Justin and I have a special bond, sure. He's the one who let me get to know him while you pushed me away, insisting you didn't want me." Airiana was a fireball when she was pissed off and now was no exception. Seeing her like this turned him on but Jarrod was sure she wouldn't allow his distraction.

"I thought we already went over all of this," Justin grumbled, standing behind Airiana. Yeah, they had but Jarrod was having trouble remembering Airiana was in love with them both.

Jarrod sighed, "We have been over this," he admitted. "This is on me."

"No," Airiana shouted, her anger ramping up. "This is on all of us. You need to stop putting up walls, Jarrod. I love you, period. I don't love Justin more or even differently than you. I love you both the same, so you need to knock it off and accept the fact if I let Justin comfort me, it doesn't mean I'm shutting you out."

"Understood." Jarrod nodded.

"This jealousy crap ends now," Justin ordered. "We

both want the same thing here, Jarrod. Our goal is to keep Airi and Milo safe—at all costs."

"Agreed," Jarrod said. They were both right and he needed to get his head on straight before he completely fucked up the best thing to ever happen to him.

"I'll catch a flight back home," Holden said. "I need to be with Slade and Ivy. She's going out of her mind with all of this."

"Let us know what you need," Justin said. "Jarrod will arrange for our lawyer to head over to the station now."

"Thanks guys." Holden pulled Airiana in for a quick hug. "You stay safe and call if you need anything, Airi."

She smile and nodded. "Tell Ivy I love her and I'll call as soon as I can."

"Will do," Holden said on his way out.

"What now?" Airiana whispered. "If we can't go home, what do we do?"

"I say we stay here for now," Justin offered. "Let's lay low and see how things play out. Maybe they'll catch the person behind Summers's murder and then we can go home and things can go back to normal." Airiana seemed sullen and Jarrod could almost read her mind. If he had to guess, their girl was worried they would rescind their offer to move in with them. That was already a done deal though, whether she was ready or not, she and Milo were already moved in with him and Justin.

Justin seemed to see she was struggling with something and he pulled her back into his body. "Out with it, honey," he ordered. Jarrod wasn't sure Airiana was going to share, so he decided to throw her words back at her.

Jarrod wrapped her in his arms and smiled, "You need to stop putting up walls, Airiana. I love you, period." She smiled up at him and nodded.

"When you say things are going to go back to normal, do you mean the way things were or the way things are now?" She turned to face Justin, wanting him to clarify what he had said.

Justin chuckled and shot Jarrod a look that told him he was about to lay it all out on the table for their girl. "We told you before that it's already a done deal, honey. Your and Milo's stuff has been moved to our place and when we get home, that will be our new normal. You are ours now, honey—you and Milo," Justin said.

"Thank you," she whispered. "So we stay here and wait out the killer?" Jarrod wanted to laugh at how silly the whole thing sounded, as if they were stuck in a bad movie trying to figure out who done it but this was their lives.

"Let's just let the dust settle and then we can decide what to do next, together—as a team," Jarrod said.

"Well, if we're voting on stuff," Justin teased.

"No," Airiana said. "I always seem to be outnumbered when there is a vote." Jarrod and Justin both laughed at Airiana's rebuke of having a vote.

"Alright," Justin said. "But I was going to offer up a vote on what we could do to your sexy body, to make you shout out our names but if you'd rather we don't—" He let his words trail off and Jarrod loved the way

Airiana playfully tapped her chin with her finger, as if trying to decide what she wanted.

"Hmm well, if that's the case, I'm all for a good old-fashioned Democratic vote—just to be fair," she teased. Justin hauled Airiana over his shoulder and carried her squealing and giggling back to their room. Jarrod followed behind them, all for whatever Justin had planned. From the sinful way Airiana looked up at Jarrod, she was on board too.

AIRIANA

It had been two weeks since Holden delivered the news of Cole's death and Airi felt as though she was going stir crazy. She wanted to get home and get back to her life but every time she brought the subject up with either of the guys, they shot her down, giving her some excuse about business keeping them in Colorado. She knew they were full of shit but she didn't want to call them on it. Airi appreciated that they wanted to keep her and Milo safe but she was starting to feel like hiding away at their cabin was over kill.

She had called Ivy daily to check in on her and was happy to hear her pregnancy was going well. Airi wished she could be there for her sister but she knew Holden and Slade were taking good care of her. Slade was released after questioning since there was no way he was involved in Cole's murder.

Her ex's death was confirmed a homicide and she hated knowing someone took his life. He might not have treated her well. Hell, he was a complete ass but he was still Milo's father. If it wasn't for Cole, she wouldn't have her son and a part of her would always be grateful to him, for that reason alone.

The local authorities had been out to the cabin to question her and the guys, as a formality. They were obviously out of the state when Cole was murdered but the police were looking for any possible leads. She wished she could have been of more help. Airi just wanted to put this whole nightmare behind them so they could go home. She was learning to trust and not fear the future the three of them were building together, and it felt damn good.

Milo seemed to love the guys almost as much as she did, and they couldn't seem to get enough of her son. Justin and Jarrod took on so many of her daily rituals with Milo, she was starting to feel useless. Watching the three of them at bath time was her favorite. She wasn't sure who was taking the bath. By the time they finished up in the bathroom all three of her guys were soaked and it always made her giggle. After bath time, the guys would give Milo his bottle and read him bedtime stories until he fell asleep on top of one of them. They always insisted she take some time to herself—read or take a bath and she had to admit, she liked being pampered.

Watching the two of them with Milo made her long for things she knew were too soon for her to hope for. She knew they would be fantastic fathers but she wondered if they wanted that with her. It was easy to love Milo but would they want him or any child, for that matter long term? They hadn't yet broached the subject of children and why would they? It had only been a few weeks since they had been together. Everything between the three of them was so new, Airi didn't want to chance asking questions or pushing for answers. She worried she wouldn't like their answers and that wasn't something she was ready to face. Sure, when they admitted they were in love with her, she explained she and Milo were a package deal but she still worried the guys would get tired of playing house and then where would she be?

Airi sat on the patio watching the three of them playing in the yard and every time Milo giggled at being chased by either Justin or Jarrod, her heart felt as though it skipped a beat. "Hey," Justin said. He sat down next to her and pulled her legs across his lap. She loved the way they were both constantly touching her, as if needing the contact.

"Hey yourself," she sassed.

"We got news today that I need to fly to California on business," Justin said. His tone was so matter of fact, she worried he was giving her the brush off but Airi knew better. She was still dealing with so many insecurities Cole had instilled in her. She needed to remember Justin and Jarrod were nothing like her ex. But, old habits were hard to break.

"How long will you guys be gone?" she whispered.

"Jarrod's not going," Justin said. "He'll stay here with you and Milo, honey." Airi knew Jarrod was staying behind for her sake but honestly, there had been no further threats since Cole was found dead and they couldn't just hide away from life.

"That's crazy," she insisted. "You guys always travel together. Now shouldn't be any different. Milo and I can just catch a plane back home and get settled at your place while you two are in California."

"No," Jarrod said, joining them on the patio. "There is no fucking way we are leaving you unprotected, baby." Airi looked between them at the determined looks on each of their faces and she knew better than to argue her point. They were two of the most stubborn men she had ever met, especially when it came to her and Milo. Still, she needed to try.

"It's been two weeks since Cole was found dead and nothing has happened. No threats, no one is coming after me. When does this end? When do the four of us get to go back to our lives and stop looking over our backs?" Airi asked. Jarrod looked at his brother and they did the whole talking without talking thing she was starting to hate.

"What?" she asked. "What aren't the two of you telling me?" She pulled free from Justin, knowing she was sending him a clear message. She needed answers and they were keeping something from her; something she was most likely not going to like hearing.

"We got a call from the private investigator we hired, to get us information on your ex," Jarrod said.

"But he's dead, why would you still be investigating him?" Airi asked.

"Let him finish, honey," Justin whispered. Airi nodded and waited Jarrod out.

"I had him looking into who would want your ex dead, you know besides everyone he hurt in life. My investigator said the police found something on the scene they didn't bother to mention to us. And well, it involves you, baby." Jarrod whispered the last part.

Airi gasped, "What does Cole's death have to do with me?" she asked.

"Holden was right," Justin said. "Whoever murdered your ex is connected to you in some way. There was a handwritten note found at the crime scene, with your name on it."

Airi tried to think of people she and Cole had in common and there weren't many. Cole was a loner and made her live the same way. He insisted she give up friends and even finished destroying her hopes of ever reuniting with her sister. It was one of his ways to keep her under his thumb. Friends would have convinced her to leave him. They would have reported him for physically hurting her and Cole wouldn't allow that.

"Why weren't we told about the note? If it had my name on it, why wasn't it given to me?" Airi asked.

"It's evidence, honey," Justin said. She could tell he wanted to pull her back down on his lap but he was giving her space to process this new information. Jarrod stood by her side but gave her the same space. She loved how they were so protective but she needed to work this out on her own. Still, it felt good to have them surrounding her with their silent support.

"We have been able to find out what the letter said," Jarrod offered.

"Tell me," she ordered.

"It simply said, 'You're next.' and we can't let that happen," Jarrod murmured. "God baby, we just found you. We can't lose you now." Jarrod didn't stop himself this time, he pulled her into his body and wrapped her tightly in his arms. Justin stood behind her, framing her completely with their bodies.

"Who would want to kill both you and your ex, honey?" Justin asked. Airi shook her head, not knowing the answer to his question. She looked out into the yard to where Milo was playing with a ball the guys got for him. The thought of leaving him made her feel physically ill. She had grown up without parents and the idea of leaving her baby to fend for himself gutted her.

"I can't think of a single person who would want us both dead. Cole wasn't the nicest person but who would want to go as far as to murder him?" Airi questioned.

Jarrod chuckled. "Well, you're looking at two of those people now, baby," he said. "After what he did to you, I know I'd want at least five minutes in a room with the guy."

"Same, honey," Justin said from behind her. "He treated you like shit and that is unacceptable. But, you're right in wondering who would go as far as to murder him and want to come after you. There isn't a single person who comes to mind?" Justin asked.

"No," she sobbed. "What happens to Milo if this person catches up to me and makes good on their promise?" She really didn't mean to ask her question aloud but she had and judging by the murderous expressions on her guy's faces, they didn't like the idea either.

"That won't fucking happen," Jarrod yelled. Milo looked up from where he was playing to see what all the commotion was about and Jarrod swore. "Sorry, baby. I won't ever let anyone get close enough to hurt you or Milo." Jarrod turned away from her to scoop up Milo as he ran to them. Her son had stopped to pick a buttercup and he handed it to her, smiling. Airi wiped at her tears and giggled at the way he kept trying to put it under her nose for her to smell.

"Thank you, baby," she gushed, taking the tiny yellow flower from his pudgy hand. Milo wrapped his arms around Jarrod's neck and Airi watched as he kissed the toddler's cheek, loving the bond that had formed between her guys in just a few short weeks.

"This is what happens to Milo, honey," Justin said. "We love him as if he's our own and we'd never let anything bad happen to him—to either of you. That is why I'm going away on business by myself. You and Milo need one of us with you right now."

"I hate that I'm making your lives more difficult," she admitted. "You two didn't sign up for someone with so much baggage."

"We signed up to be with you, Airiana," Jarrod whispered. "We got exactly what we wanted and I, for one, wouldn't change one thing about us." Jarrod pulled her up his body, kissing her mouth and Milo seemed to like all the hugging and kissing going around. He framed her face with his tiny hand and leaned in to kiss Airi's nose, causing them all to laugh.

"So, when do you have to leave?" she asked Justin. She knew she would have to resign herself to the fact that they were going to do exactly what they pleased, especially when it came to her.

"Tonight," he said. "Want to help me pack?" He pulled her back against his body and Airi knew he had more than just packing in mind. They had never really discussed one-on-one time between her and the guys and she wondered just how this was going to work.

"Um," she looked up at Jarrod, who was still holding Milo, hoping he'd give her some guidance.

He chuckled and bent to gently kiss her mouth. "It's fine, Airiana. I'll hang out here with Milo and you go help my brother pack. We are going to both have our private time with you and we are fine with that. My brother and I share but we also know we need to build our individual relationships with you. It will only make us a stronger threesome if we do."

"Besides," Justin added, "You and Jarrod will have the next few days together, just the two of you, and I will want to play catch up when I get back from California." He bobbed his eyebrows at her, causing her to giggle. Airi enthusiastically nodded, liking the idea of spending alone time with each of her guys. It would give her and Jarrod a chance to get to know each other a little better. She and Justin seemed to have a head start in that department, and some one-on-one time with Jarrod might be exactly what they both needed.

———

Justin left for his trip, promising to be a quick as possible and a part of Airi felt an inexplicable sadness he wasn't going to be around. She felt greedy for wanting them both with her all the time but was also realistic enough to know that couldn't be a reality.

Jarrod had taken Milo for his bath as he usually did but he seemed a little off without Justin being around. Airi chalked it up to the two of them doing everything together and Jarrod feeling a little lost without his brother around. But a part of her wondered if he was nervous about the two of them being alone together.

She and Justin had formed a bond, even a friendship, since she had started working for Grayson Industries. They had even been out on a few dates to eat but she didn't realize that was what they were at the time. She naively believed Justin was just being kind to her but now she saw he was trying to get to know her. Jarrod never let his personal life mingle with his private one and that meant keeping Airi at arm's length. They had never really shared any alone time on a personal level, just the two of them. Their time alone usually involved her being called into his office and him going over what he needed from her work wise. Sure, she had fantasized he'd call her into his office to demand things from her personally but that never happened. Not until his hand was forced by finding her on the jet after Justin had insisted she tag along on their trip.

Justin seemed to be the glue that held them all together. He was the one who had a relationship with each of them. Justin was the one insisting they spend time together and he was right. It would only make them a stronger unit if they did.

"He's asleep," Jarrod whispered from the doorway

to their bedroom. Airi had decided to use her free time to take a bath and to slip into some sexy lingerie. The guys had done some shopping for her and Milo since they were spending more time than anticipated in Colorado. She had drawers full of sexy scraps of lace and she was sure both of her men would permanently keep her in a constant state of undress if it wasn't for Milo and work getting in the way of their plans.

She wasn't sure if she had chosen to wear something Jarrod would approve of until she saw the way his eyes flared when he looked her up and down. "What's all this?" he asked. She loved how he was almost shy around her. Jarrod was usually so in control —her Dom but tonight he was shy and almost seemed nervous.

"It's just me," she whispered to him, reaching her hand out, hoping he'd take her offer.

"I know Airi but I just feel somewhat out of sorts, with it being just the two of us. I'm used to having Justin around." He reached for her outstretched hand and pulled her closer. Airi willingly let him wrap her in his arms, hoping she could give him some reassurances that she wanted him, even needed him, just as much as she did Justin. She knew Jarrod had issues with his role in their relationship and that was the last thing she wanted resurfacing.

"Have you ever had a relationship without Justin?" she questioned. Airi worried she was being too pushy, asking such a personal question but she had been an open book for them both. She knew the guys had shared women, they admitted that freely but she wondered just how many one-on-one relationships either of them had had.

"I've been on a few solo dates but never a relationship, per say." Hearing Jarrod admit he had never had a solo relationship did strange things to her heart.

"I'll be your first then," she said.

"Yes," he breathed against her skin, burying his head against her neck. "You okay with that, Airiana?" he asked, seeming to be unsure of himself again. She had to admit this new, shy Jarrod melted her defenses. Airi liked his dominant side but the way he seemed to follow her lead now turned her on. It gave her a new boldness she had never had. Jarrod made her feel sexy and wanted and even self-assured and it was all new for her.

"I'm more than okay with it, Jarrod. I like that I'm your first solo relationship. I like that I'm the first woman you and Justin have shared in your home. I'm the first woman you have both chosen to live with and build a life with." she said.

Jarrod kissed his way down her neck, "You're the first woman we've fallen in love with," Jarrod whispered against her skin.

"Yes, she breathed. "You both are the first men I've ever loved," she admitted. She was being completely honest. Airi had never been in love with Cole. Sure, she thought she was in love with him at the time but she was wrong. Being with Jarrod and Justin taught her just what love was supposed to look like. Now that she knew the real thing, Airi could confidently say she never loved Cole. She'd forever love the child they created together but that was the only kind thought she could muster for her ex.

"You never loved him?" Jarrod asked, as if being able to read her thoughts.

"No," she whispered. "I thought I did at the time but loving you and Justin now, it's not the same." Jarrod smiled against her sensitive skin and gently bit down, causing her to yelp.

"I like being in your list of firsts, Airiana," he whispered. "I can't speak for Justin but I plan on being your last love too. I want you, Airiana," he said. Jarrod kissed his way back down her neck, leaving gentle little bite marks on her skin as he went. It always turned Airi on the way he wasn't very gentle with her. She was finding she liked things a little rough and Jarrod never disappointed her.

"Then take me," she whispered. Jarrod didn't seem to need any further invitation. He pulled the scraps of fabric from her body with ease, leaving her completely bare to his gaze. Every inch of her body that his eyes roamed felt as though he had personally touched her there. Her whole body heated and she was literally panting with anticipation.

"There's my beautiful girl," Jarrod soothed. It sounded as though he was talking to a wild animal and hell, maybe that was exactly what she looked like. But, she didn't care. She wanted him with everything she had.

"I'm going to tie you down to our bed and eat that sweet pussy of mine, until you can't remember your own name, Airiana," he purred. Words seemed to fail her, all she could do was nod her head, giving her agreement. This Jarrod, the Dom who like to control her body, mind and spirit, was her favorite.

"The words, Airiana," he ordered, causing her to jump. "I need the words."

Airi smiled up at him, "Yes, Jarrod. I want for you to tie me to our bed and help me to forget my name," she sassed. He swatted her ass on his way to the nightstand to get the hand cuffs. Jarrod ordered her up onto their bed and she quickly complied. She wanted so badly to please him, to show him she was just as much his as she was both of theirs. She had spent the morning alone with Justin helping him to pack and obeying his every command in bed. Now, it was Jarrod's turn and she planned on wiping every stitch of uncertainty from his mind about how much she wanted him.

"Good girl," he praised. Airi spread out on the mattress and he secured both of her wrists to the metal headboard. "Spread your legs for me, baby," he ordered. Airi complied and watched as Jarrod worked his way down her body, securing each of her ankles to the bed posts, effectively spreading her completely open to his every whim. Her core ached for relief and she knew Jarrod would find her pussy drenched with her need for him.

Airi pulled against her restraints needing to move, wanting to watch what Jarrod planned next for her but she already knew. She held her breath in anticipation, only releasing it when Jarrod ran two fingers through her wet folds.

"Airiana," he breathed. She could feel his warm breath on her pussy and it was nearly her undoing. She moaned out his name just from the anticipation of what he had planned for her. Jarrod was always so creative when it came to making her come. Airi couldn't wait. He chuckled against her sensitive pussy and licked her throbbing clit. She bucked and pulled against the handcuffs, loving the little bites of pain that was making the pleasure Jarrod was giving her so much better.

"You like that, don't you, baby?" he asked. "The way the pain makes it all better. You are my kinky girl, aren't you?" Airi moaned again, not answering his question.

Instead she begged, "Please, Jarrod. I need to come." She didn't care if she sounded out of control with need, she was. He was turning her inside out and making her wait was all part of his seductive plan. Turnabout would be fair play and as soon as it was her turn to touch and taste him, she would drive him out of his mind.

"I can't deny you, sweet girl. I'm going to let you come this time and when you do, I want my name on those sexy lips of yours," he ordered. Airi nodded and laid her head back, waiting for him to make good on his promise. But she knew better than to doubt him, he always did.

Jarrod licked his way back into her sensitive folds and this time, he didn't stop until she felt as though she was soaring through space and could actually touch the stars. She came around his greedy mouth and he gently led her back down, kissing and sucking his way up her body. When she finally regained all her senses, Airi realized Jarrod had stripped and was stroking his cock, as if awaiting her attention. She smiled up at him, licking her lips, wanting to taste his cock. Airi patiently waited his instructions, hoping she'd have her chance to drive Jarrod even half as crazy as he had driven her. She liked when Jarrod told her exactly what he wanted from her.

"Tell me what you want, Airiana," he ordered. She didn't hide her smile. He knew exactly what she was going to ask for and from the smirk on his gorgeous face, Jarrod was ready and willing to give it to her.

"I want to taste you please, Jarrod." She pulled at the handcuffs, as if trying to reach for him and cried out in pain. "I need to touch you too, please," Airi begged. Jarrod's eyes flared with need and she knew that was exactly what he was hoping she would say. He unlocked her hands from the headboard and removed the cuffs from around her ankles, giving her free access to his body. Usually, Jarrod like to keep her cuffed or tied up when he took her body, this was new for him. Justin liked to have her touch him and usually ordered her to do so but Jarrod didn't like giving up any of his control while he fucked his way into her body.

"Thank you," she whispered. "May I touch you, Jarrod?" she waited him out and finally he nodded. She liked how shy Jarrod was making an appearance in bed but this was new territory for her.

"I need for you to touch me, Airiana. Show me you're my girl," he ordered. She didn't hesitate, knowing Jarrod struggled with where he fit between her and Justin. Jarrod held the other half of her heart and he needed to know that.

"I love you, Jarrod," she said, slipping her arms around his neck. "It's just you and me right now. Let me love you," she offered. Jarrod nodded and lifted her body up over his cock, allowing her to slide down his shaft inch by inch. It was almost too much, the feel of him entering her body, the way he maintained eye contact, his hands roaming her sensitive nipples—it was an overload to her senses.

"Fuck, you feel so good, Airiana," he whispered against her shoulder. When she was fully seated on his cock, he ordered her to move and she did, never taking her eyes off his. It was as if he could see straight into her soul. She knew she was looking directly into the sun but she didn't care. Airi couldn't seem to look away.

"Like this?" she questioned, almost sliding completely off his cock. Jarrod moaned her name, telling her she was doing exactly what he liked.

"Yes," he hissed his response. "Don't stop, baby. I'm going to come," he commanded. She rode his shaft, loving the freedom he was giving her to control her every move and in turn, his pending orgasm.

"Do you know how important you are to me, Jarrod?" She looked him directly in the eyes and when he tried to look away from her, she framed his face with her hands caressing his jaw. "Tell me you know how much I love you, Jarrod," she ordered. She refused to let him hide. Airi held his handsome gaze, riding his cock, until he finally nodded.

"I know, baby," he admitted. "I see it every time you look at me," he breathed.

"You hold the other half of my heart, Jarrod," she cried out, another orgasm ripped through her body but this time, Jarrod followed her over. He pumped deep into her core, holding her hips firmly in his big hands, finally taking what he needed from her.

"Tell me you are mine, Airiana," he ordered.

She nodded, "I'm yours, Jarrod," she agreed. "I love you so much." Jarrod pulled her down onto the bed with him and they laid there for so long, Airi thought he had fallen asleep.

"I love you too, Airiana," he whispered and pulled her against his body. She was his and Jarrod finally knew it and that was all she needed.

JUSTIN

J ustin was exhausted. His trip took an extra day and he was ready to get back to Colorado to meet up with Jarrod and go over every detail of his many business meetings. He was also hoping his brother and Airi would have found time to connect while he was gone.

Justin had called in nightly to check on Airi and Jarrod and once in a while he caught Milo still awake. Although the toddler's gibberish was hard to understand, he loved hearing his little voice. He knew giving Jarrod time alone with their girl was the best way to help them bond but it was killing him to be away from them all. Honestly, his business could have been done by teleconference but he wouldn't tell his brother that. He saw that Jarrod was having trouble struggling with his relationship with Airi. There was no way for them to move forward if Jarrod couldn't form some sort of bond with her. Sure, he knew Jarrod loved Airi but he still saw the jealousy in his brother's eyes sometimes when Jarrod didn't think anyone was watching.

After he got out to California, Justin put out one fire after another and he was actually happy he made the trip. Judging from his phone calls, it was successful on all fronts because Jarrod and Airi seemed closer than ever. When he got the chance to talk to Airi alone, she'd gush about her time with Jarrod and Justin had to admit he wasn't jealous. He was relieved more than anything the two had found their way but he was never jealous.

When he called home last night, Jarrod told him he got a call from Holden, saying they were needed back at the home office. He hated the idea they were possibly taking Airi back into a dangerous situation but they really had no choice. They all knew sooner or later they would have to return to their lives. They couldn't hide out in Colorado forever, although he was hoping for just a few more days there. He'd love to go fishing again but decided that would have to wait for another trip west.

Holden had also done some digging and although they still didn't know who was after Airiana, the local authorities assumed it was someone from her past. They were looking into all the foster families Airi had lived with. She submitted a full list, disclosing the names of all her past families. Justin hated how he was possibly exposing her to whatever trouble was tracking her down but she seemed excited to get back home. Airi said she missed her sister and wanted to get Milo back to his regular routine. Justin had to admit he was looking forward to having Airi and Milo living with him and Jarrod full time. He loved that they would be a part of each other's daily routine and when they all left to go home in the evening, he wouldn't have to wonder what Airi was doing every night. Hell, he used to spend most of his nights rock hard thinking about her but now she would be lying beside him in bed. He wondered how he had gotten so lucky but he didn't like to chance fate. All he knew was Airi belonged to Jarrod and him and that wouldn't change.

They decided to all meet at the airport to save Justin some traveling time and he was grateful. While the jet refueled, he checked messages, noting he had thirteen missed calls from Holden. He decided to take a few minutes to call him back and didn't count it as a good sign his friend answered on the first ring.

"It's about time," Holden grumbled.

"Well, it's good to hear from you too, man." Justin felt he was poking the bear but he didn't care. It had been a damn long day and it wasn't over yet.

"Is Airi with you?" Holden asked. Justin stood, knowing that Holden was calling about Airi had him worried.

"No, she's on her way to the airport now with Jarrod," he said. "Why, what's going on?"

"The officer in charge of Cole's homicide case called Ivy today, asking for Airi. He said they had a lead and wanted to know if the name Jimmy meant anything to Airi." Justin knew from Holden's tone he was aware of Airi's history with Jimmy, which was fine with him since he didn't want to get into it.

"I know all about that asshole, Holden," Justin confirmed. "What does he have to do with any of the shit going on with Cole?" he asked.

"Well, it seems this Jimmy guy wasn't able to let Airi go. They tracked him down and he all but admitted to murdering Cole but then he disappeared," Holden said.

"What the hell do you mean, he just disappeared?" Justin questioned. "How did the police lose him?"

"I have no idea man but it seems Jimmy just got up and walked out of there and hasn't been seen or heard from since," Holden said. "They are looking for him but he's gone."

"There's more, isn't there?" Justin asked. Holden sighed into the other end of the line. "Just get it all out," Justin commanded.

"In the interview when they were questioning him, he admitted to being the baby's father. Airi's baby—the one she lost." Holden paused, as if waiting him out.

"Fuck," Justin swore.

"Yeah, well he said he wanted Airi and his baby but his parents were the ones keeping them apart. He said his father sent Airi away and he lost touch with her but he wants her back and has been looking for Airi all this time," Holden all but whispered the last part.

"No fucking way," Justin growled. "There is no fucking way he will ever get his hands on her again. Airi said she was taken out of that home when she told her case worker that Jimmy was forcing himself on her. He's a fucking liar," Justin said.

"I know, man. Ivy told Slade and I the whole story. The officer said this guy didn't seem to have all his faculties about him. He wasn't playing with a full deck and he's worried if you bring Airi home, he'll have his chance to get to her."

"Jarrod and I will increase security around the office and our home. We won't let Airi out of our sight. She and Milo will be well protected, you don't have to worry about that," Justin offered.

"I believe you, Justin. I just thought you'd like to know what you guys are up against," Holden said.

"I appreciate it, Holden. I really do. We will be back in town tonight late. I'll have Airi call Ivy tomorrow to let her know she's safe." Justin ended the call just in time to find Airi and Jarrod boarding the plane with Milo in tow. He was going to have to explain his phone call but first he needed to hold his girl and make sure she hadn't forgotten him. Justin kissed Milo's little head and pulled Airi against his body, kissing into her mouth. He didn't let her even catch her breath before wrapping his arms around her, squeezing her tight.

"I missed you so fucking much, honey," he whispered. Justin nodded to Jarrod and his brother smiled at him.

"What, you didn't miss me too?" Jarrod teased.

"I did but I think I'll hold off on your hug and kiss," Justin said, making Airi giggle. God, he missed her laugh. He missed everything about his girl. Justin sat down and pulled Airi onto his lap; Jarrod and Milo sat down in the seat next to him.

"Who was on the phone?" Airi questioned. She

never missed a beat and there would be no hiding the truth from her.

"Holden," Justin admitted.

"Everything alright back home?" Jarrod asked.

"Well, yes and no," Justin said. "Everything is fine with your sister and the company is good but Holden called to give us a heads up that the officer in charge of your ex's murder case might have a lead on who might want to hurt you." Seeing the frightened look on Airi's face nearly did him in. Here he didn't have her back in his arms even five minutes and he had to deliver bad news.

"Who?" she whispered.

"Jimmy," Justin said. He hated that he sounded so matter of fact but there was no other way. "He was brought in for questioning a couple days ago and basically admitted to everything, including wanting you back. But he got away somehow." He looked over to Jarrod, noting the murderous look on his brother's face.

He had to hand it to Jarrod, he kept it together while holding Milo. "How could they just let him walk away?" Jarrod asked. Milo had no clue as to what they were talking about. He continued to play with his favorite stuffed bunny while they all tried to calmly discuss the news Holden delivered.

"Holden wasn't sure," Justin said. "He did say they are looking for this Jimmy and warned us if we brought Airi home, she might be in danger." Airi looked between the two of them and instead of the tears and upset he expected, he saw only her resolve and strength looking back at him.

"I'm done hiding," Airi said. "While I've enjoyed our little trip and staying in your beautiful house here in Colorado, I want to go home. I want to see Ivy and get back to work. Milo needs stability and a schedule and we need to settle into our new routine, living with the two of you." Justin nodded, knowing she was right.

"Then we go home, honey," Justin agreed.

"Tell me we're increasing our security team," Jarrod questioned.

"Yep, at work and at home. I'll make the call just before we take off," Justin said. "And until they can catch this—guy," he stuttered, making Airi smile. From the amused look on her face, she knew he wanted to call Jimmy an asshole but refrained because she had already given plenty of warnings about their cursing around Milo. He was trying to be a good example around her son but not cursing was turning out to be quite the challenge.

"Until they can catch him, you will be with one of us twenty-four- seven. Got it?" Jarrod finished for him. Airi smiled and nodded.

"You know, you two are really like an old married couple," she teased. "You even finish each other's sentences." She giggled. Justin smushed her against his body and kissed her again.

"I have a few phone calls to make. Why don't you get Milo settled before we take off?" Justin asked. Airi nodded and stood, taking Milo from Jarrod and heading back to the bedroom at the back of the plane.

She shut the door and Jarrod turned to face him. Justin knew his brother was going to have a ton of questions but they didn't have time for all of them. So, Jarrod went with the one question that was on both of their minds. "Will we be able to keep her safe, man?" he whispered.

"I have no idea," Justin admitted. "But I hope to fuck we can."

JARROD

Two weeks had flown by in the blink of an eye and Jarrod was sure he had never felt more at peace in his life. It had taken him and Justin a damn long time to find the right woman to fit between the two of them but Airiana did perfectly. She and Milo had become his and Justin's whole life and a few months prior he would have never imagined it to be a possibility.

After the initial shock of the three of them being an item and the circulation of news they were all living together, the office gossip mill seemed to settle down. He and Justin worried Airiana wouldn't be able to handle some of the nasty comments and stares from some of the other employees but she handled them all like a champ.

Everything was going along almost too perfectly and Jarrod was constantly looking over his shoulder, waiting for the other shoe to drop, so to speak. He hated living that way and hoped that sooner or later this Jimmy asshole would show his hand so they could catch him and put him away. He wanted to be done with watching over their shoulders and he could tell that Airiana and Justin were feeling the same way.

They were keeping such a short leash on Airiana, she was starting to show the effects. She cried all the damn time. If Milo picked a weed out of the grass for her, his girl would break down in tears. Jarrod worried the stress was starting to get to her and he wondered just how much more she would be willing to take. Airiana was also giving him more sass than she used to but he was sure it was an attribute of hers becoming more comfortable around the two of them and not her stress levels on the rise. She was the perfect package—sexy as sin and was fun and witty to boot, really keeping them on their toes. Airiana would never be boring.

She walked into his office and flopped down on the sofa that sat in front of his desk. "Hi," he said, not bothering to hide his smirk. She was in quite a mood all morning and from the look on her beautiful face, nothing had changed. She blew out her breath, effectively blowing a strand of her blond hair that had escaped her messy bun back from her face, causing him to laugh.

"None of this is funny, Jarrod," she grouched. "There are armed guards upstairs watching my toddler." Jarrod quickly sobered. She was right, not one bit of their situation was humorous.

"I know, baby and I'm sorry," he offered but Airiana wasn't having it. She wasn't looking for apologies or a quick brush off. If he knew his girl, and he did, she was up to something and he was not going to like it. "Spill it, Airiana. What are you really doing here? Milo has been under guard since we returned. What's really bothering you?"

Airiana huffed out another dramatic sigh and this time, he stifled his own laugh. She was really selling it, whatever "it" was. "I want to go to lunch," she spat. "I want to get my nails and hair done. I want a fucking life."

"Well, we will have all of that again soon, baby. We just need to be patient and let the police do their jobs. They will catch this asshole who's trying to hurt you, and we will be back to doing all of our fun, normal, everyday things." Jarrod watched her, knowing that wasn't going to be the end of her tirade.

"This doesn't seem to be affecting you and Justin like it has been me," she sassed. "You two go out to lunch and do whatever it is you have to do. I'm the one stuck under lock and key." She pouted and it was probably the cutest thing Jarrod had ever seen. He smiled at her and God, he wanted to give her everything she had been asking him for but he couldn't.

"No, Airiana. I'm sorry but whatever you're dreaming up, the answer is no," he said, pointing his finger in her direction.

"Can't I just have one little thing?" she begged.

"No," he barked.

"I just want a cheese steak—you know one filled with gooey cheese and meat, smothered in onions," she moaned the last word, making him instantly hard. Here she was, talking about cheese steak subs and just her description of them was making him hard.

"Fuck, Airiana," he complained. "Why do you make me so crazy?" he asked.

She shrugged and smiled. Airiana knew exactly what she was doing to him. "Is it working?" she sassed.

"No," he lied. "Alright, yes. But, you can't just go traipsing around town for a sub. It's just too dangerous. Justin and I have a meeting here in ten minutes and we can't go with you." She pouted again, melting the last of his defenses. "Fuck," he swore again. "You do that better than Milo," he teased. She laughed and stood.

"How about if I promise to stay close and be a good girl? I'll even take two guards with me," she said. Airiana crossed her heart with her fingers and pasted on her best smile.

"No," he said again. "I can send someone else out for your sub but I won't have you leaving this office. Am I clear?" Jarrod knew he sounded like an asshole but he didn't care. He wouldn't take any chances with her safety and he knew Justin felt the same way and would agree with him. Hell, she was probably going to go to him next. The thought was almost amusing. Airiana crossed her arms over her chest, accentuating her impressive cleavage and turned to leave his office without another word.

"I love you, Airiana," he shouted after her.

"Mm-hm," she sassed back, causing him to laugh. She was definitely trouble and Jarrod loved every minute of it.

AIRIANA

Airi found her purse and jacket and quickly went to the hallway where her guards were supposed to be but there was no sign of either of them. If she was going to outright defy Jarrod's orders, she could at least take her security detail with her. She was angry with Jarrod for not agreeing to her plan but she wouldn't go off and do something that could get her killed. She walked down to the break room, hoping they would be in there having coffee or just taking some down time but they weren't there either. Instead of tracking them down and wasting even more time, she decided to run to the sub shop just around the corner by herself. She was sure she'd be back long before anyone even missed her. In fact, that was the plan because having to deal with Jarrod's anger wasn't her idea of a good time. He would never hurt her, not like Cole did but he could sulk for days if he was mad enough.

It only took her five minutes to walk to the shop and

by the time she got there, she was starving. All she could think about during her morning meetings was a cheese steak sub. Airi placed their orders, getting the guys each their favorite subs and was walking back to the office, when a man stepped from the back alley she always cut through.

"Excuse me," she said, trying to sidestep him but he slipped in front of her, blocking her path forward. She looked up and saw the menacing way he looked at her and knew exactly whom she had run in to—Jimmy. Sure, he was older, they both were but she would never forget his eyes or the way he looked at her. It was a cross between love and hate and always sent a shiver down Airi's spine.

"Jimmy," she whispered. "Please don't do this," she begged. His laugh was enough to have her putting up her defenses. Airi knew if she just stood there, Jimmy would win. There was no way she could fight him; he was so much bigger than she was. Her only hope was to run and if she was lucky, be faster than Jimmy. He grabbed her arm, almost as if he could read her thoughts and pulled her against his body. He smelled like day old whisky and cigarettes, reminding her of her childhood but not in a good, stroll down memory lane, kind of way.

"I've missed you, Airi," he whispered in her ear. She dropped the bag of subs and pulled her arm free from his hold.

"Don't touch me," she growled.

"Or what, honey?" he taunted.

"Or I'll be forced to do this." Airi reached into her

purse and pulled the mace from her bag. Her sister insisted she carry it with her, being a single mom living over a bar and she had to admit she was grateful for having it. She shot it right in Jimmy's face and turned to run.

"You bitch," he shouted, lunging for her, as if guessing she was about to make a break for it. He toppled her to the ground and Airi felt a searing pain shoot through her head after it hit the street. The last thought that ran through her mind was of her sweet little boy and the men who she loved, just before everything around her went dark.

———

Airi felt as though her entire world was spinning off kilter. Her head hurt and she was sure she had a concussion. A new wave of nausea overtook her and she thought she was going to be sick.

"Oh good, look who's awake." The voice she still heard in her nightmares now rang through to her and she reluctantly blinked her eyes open against the harsh bright light. His laugh sounded just as evil as it had years ago when she was just a young girl and she knew exactly who she was dealing with.

"Jimmy," she groggily whispered.

"Well, well Princess. It's about time you woke up and paid me some attention. Hell, I've been trying to get your fucking attention for years now." Jimmy ran his hand up her arm and she wanted to tell him to keep his fucking hands to himself but she didn't have the strength. Airi's eyes focused and she saw the face of the boy who did unspeakable things to her years ago. That boy was now a man but she could tell it was him. He had the same shifty eyes that looked her over like she was his next meal. He had the same laugh and when he touched her, he invoked the same feeling of disgust and loathing deep within her gut.

"Why?" she asked. Her voice cracked and she knew Jimmy was taking a good deal of pleasure in the fact she sounded so afraid. She looked around the tiny room, realizing she didn't recognize her surroundings. Airi was laying on a small bed, her wrists handcuffed to the metal bed post and she struggled against her bonds. Every movement elicited a sharp pain in either her head or her arms and she finally calmed herself enough to lay still, minimizing her agony.

His chuckle sent shivers down her spine. "Why what baby?" he questioned. "Why am I trying to get your attention? Why have I wasted years of my fucking life, trying to get you to finally notice me?" Jimmy ran the pad of his thumb over her cheek and down her jaw and she gagged, remembering all the evil things he did to her in the past.

"Aww honey, just relax," he ordered. "I've done all of this for you, baby. I've been watching you for years now. Hell, I'm the one who made it possible for you and that fucking idiot, Cole to meet. All that time wasted and he didn't do a fucking thing right," Jimmy complained.

"What do you mean? How did you make it possible that we met?" she questioned. Airi's head throbbed and she wasn't sure if she understood Jimmy because he was talking in circles or if her foggy brain wasn't keeping up. Either way, she was going to have to get herself together and come up with a plan to find her way back to Milo and the guys. She had to do it for them, if not for herself.

"You just left—you fucking left and how was I to know if you were alright? I sent Cole Summers in to keep an eye on you but he went and got you pregnant, fucking everything up," Jimmy spat.

"I left your parents foster home because you forced me to have sex with you and got me pregnant." She wanted to yell and scream at him but all she could muster was a whisper.

"You said yes," Jimmy yelled. "You fucking told me yes and not just once but over and over. I never forced you, Airi. You wanted it just as much as I did."

"That's not true," she denied his words. "You told me you would hurt those other girls. They were just little girls and you said if I didn't have sex with you, you'd force them to. How could I let you do that? You left me no choice but to agree to every disgusting thing you wanted me to do. You're sick, Jimmy. You need help." Airi gingerly shook her aching head and he laughed at her obvious discomfort.

"You tell yourself whatever you need to get through the day, honey," he teased. "I know the truth. You loved me and we created another life together but then you went and lost our baby. How could you be so careless, Airiana?" She hated hearing Jimmy talk about the baby she lost. She was only a kid herself but she was resigned to try to be a good mother for her child. Airi didn't plan for the baby but she would have never done anything to hurt her own child, she just didn't have it in her to hurt her own flesh and blood. After her miscarriage, she mourned the baby for months, feeling guilty as hell. The doctor told her she didn't do anything wrong, those things happened sometimes and it was just nature's way of making things right. She didn't understand his meaning at the time but now she did. Life had a funny way of working itself out and losing the baby was just one of those things.

"I loved that baby but not you, Jimmy. Never you. I could never love a monster," she spat, getting some of her voice back. She was starting to feel a little stronger and knew it might be her anger working in her favor but she would use every ounce of her new found strength to stand up to the bully who nearly destroyed her life.

"You're not capable of loving anyone, bitch." She wanted to laugh in his face but Airi knew it would hurt too much to do so. She loved her family, her son and God she loved Justin and Jarrod but she would never share anything so personal with Jimmy. He was her tainted past she'd rather forget but Airi knew he wouldn't let her just walk away from him.

Airi knew she needed to keep Jimmy talking to hopefully buy herself some time. "Why did you set things up between Cole and me, if you didn't want me with him?" she questioned.

"When you left me I had no choice but to keep tabs on you. After you aged out of the system, I had no way to keep an eye on you anymore, so I came up with the idea of hiring an old friend to get close to you," he admitted.

"Cole," Airi whispered.

"Yes, I went to high school with Cole Summers and he was down on his luck, so I knew he'd take me up on my offer. I set him up in the little apartment you two shared and even told him where to casually run into you. I had no idea you'd be easy and fall into bed so quickly with him." Jimmy looked at her as if he was disgusted by her, as if he had any reason to be. She didn't care what Jimmy thought of her and his upset wasn't any of her concern.

"So you set up our meeting and paid him to get close to me?" Airi felt foolish she never saw the signs but looking back, they were there. Cole acted as if he was completely disinterested in her most of the time. When she got pregnant with Milo, he became angry, almost irate towards her. That was about the time Cole started hitting her. He was never the man she thought he was and for the longest time she didn't trust herself to make any personal decisions. Until now, with the guys. They were the first leap of faith Airi took since hooking up with Cole and she was so happy she took a chance with them.

"Basically, I just never imagined you would fall into bed with him so quickly. You always were a little slut, weren't you, Airi?" He pulled her up from the bed she laid on and she was sure she was going to vomit with the sudden movement. Her arms had lost most of their feeling, which was a welcome change from the agonizing pain from every sudden movement.

"And then you went and got yourself pregnant with that brat of yours," he hissed.

"Milo isn't a brat, asshole," she yelled back. Jimmy's smile was mean and she knew she wasn't going to like whatever he was about to say.

"You weren't supposed to have him but that asshole couldn't seem to get anything right. When I confronted Cole he assured me you would lose his baby, just like you lost mine but he couldn't seem to finish the job. Sure, you landed in the hospital a few times but you never lost the brat, did you Airi?" She gasped at Jimmy's question.

"You wanted me to lose my baby?" she whispered.

"Hell, I paid that fucker to do his best to make sure you lost that kid but he never got it right did he? My baby was the one you should have had. My baby deserved to have the same chance your God awful brat has now. But my kid is dead and soon, yours will be too. I plan on handling that myself." The look on Jimmy's face told Airi he meant every word. He planned on going after Milo when he finished with her but the guys wouldn't ever let Jimmy get to her son. They would guard him with their lives, just as they had tried to do with her. But she was a fool and didn't listen to them. She thought she knew better and took off on her own, wanting her life back. Airi just never imagined Jimmy would be the one behind it all, the one chasing her down all those years, the one wanting to murder her and the people she loved. If nothing else, this all would stop with her, she'd make sure of it.

"You paid Cole to murder my baby? You're disgusting," she yelled.

Jimmy's laugh was mean. "I really don't care what you think about me or my motives, honey. It would have all been worth it too, if your brother-in-law hadn't stuck his nose where it didn't belong. After your sister and her husbands got involved, everything went to hell," he complained. "And now, you're living with your two bosses, just like your slut of a sister. Two guys, Airi," he tisked. She laughed and realized that finding his monologue funny, seemed to piss him off.

"Is that what's bothering you, Jimmy? I've found happiness and you never will—that's it right?" she taunted. He stood from the side of the bed she was on and paced the floor, telling her she had hit a nerve. Airi had to admit, she loved how he was so easily roused by her assumptions. She wondered if she kept pushing him if he'd end up making a mistake allowing her to find a way to escape, or if she'd end up pushing him too far.

"What you've found isn't happiness, it's unholy. You're just too damaged to realize what you are doing with those two men is disgusting. Poor little Airi—you want to be loved so badly you don't understand right from wrong any longer. That's where I come in, honey," he said, sitting back down on the bed. It dipped from his weight and she braced herself for whatever he was planning but he didn't make another move towards her. Jimmy just sat there, staring her down and she almost felt it was worse than if he had touched her. Waiting for his next move was excruciating.

"We'll have plenty of time to figure out our next move, Airi. First, I need to run a few errands to pick up some supplies. Then you and I are going on a little trip. I can't have your boyfriends snooping around town looking for you. We are going to get the hell out of town and then you and I are going to get reacquainted," Jimmy promised. He stood and crossed the small room, pausing in the doorway to look back at her.

"I can't wait to make you mine again, honey," he said. Airi didn't hide her sob, knowing Jimmy's threat was a promise he'd enjoy keeping.

JARROD

"Where the fuck is she, man?" he yelled his question at Justin and he could tell his brother had no clue how to answer him. He wished they had a lead, a clue, hell—a fucking breadcrumb to follow. They had nothing to go on and Airiana had been gone for five hours now. Jarrod knew every passing hour gave the asshole that had her a bigger lead and a better chance of not being found.

"I don't know, Jarrod. God, I wish we had something to go on here but I'm just as lost in all of this as you are." As soon as Jarrod got the text from that asshole, Jimmy, showing he had Airiana, they called the local authorities in to handle the case. But, they were taking forever to come up with a single lead. It was time for them to get their own security team involved, no matter the consequences.

"I've called in the team and they will be here in the next ten minutes," Justin said. "Ivy picked up Milo an hour ago from daycare, and Holden and Slade know the deal. If this asshole got to Airi, he'll probably be going after Milo next. I've sent two men from our security team home with them."

"Thank fuck," Jarrod said. "We can't take any chances with Milo; our girl will have our balls if we do."

"We've got to get her back," Justin whispered. "I don't know what we'll do if she's gone." Justin paused. Jarrod didn't want him to say anything else. He knew what could happen to Airiana and thinking of the worst case scenario wasn't an option right now. If they did, neither of them would be in the right frame of mind to help their girl.

"What the hell was she thinking? I explicitly told her not to go out for lunch and she defied me," Jarrod growled. He hated how she blatantly disregarded her own personal safety and went out to get their lunches, after he specifically told her to stay the fuck at her desk.

Getting the text of her gagged and bound to a bed, passed out from whatever that fucker Jimmy did to her, made him half crazy. She was out there, probably scared and in trouble, and they couldn't get to her. He felt helpless and every time he thought of the things that could happen to her he wanted to put his fists through a wall.

"She messed up, man—we all did. We were under the illusion everything had calmed down but we were wrong. That fucker was just biding his time, waiting for us to miss a step and when he got his chance, he took it. He took our girl and now we have to get her back. I can't live without her—I won't," Justin shouted. Jarrod knew his brother and he were on the same page.

Whatever it took, they would get Airiana back or die trying.

———

Jarrod sat back in his chair, sick and tired of having to go over the same story for the past hour. They were wasting precious time and he was sick of sitting around, talking about what happened and hypothetical situations. Their head of security, Mike Mulligan had been questioning them for what seemed like an eternity and Jarrod was ready to get his team out. The sooner they hit the pavement looking for Airiana, the sooner she would be home, in their arms.

"While I appreciate your thoroughness Mike, I think it's time we start talking strategy," Justin barked from where he paced in the corner of Jarrod's office. "Our girl is missing, an asshole named Jimmy took her and we want her back. It's really cut and dry. Just get out there and do your fucking job." Jarrod had to agree with his brother's assessment of the situation, although his delivery was a bit cold.

"What my brother is trying to say is, we've been at this for an hour. You should have the information you need to find Airiana. We appreciate you keeping us in the loop," Jarrod said. He stood and waited for Mike to do the same but he didn't make a move.

"How about you two calm the fuck down and let me do my job," Mike said. Jarrod would have found the whole scene funny under normal circumstances but nothing about Airiana's abduction was humorous.

Mike Mulligan had come highly recommended and had been the head of their security detail for almost two years. There was no way Jarrod would start questioning the guy now but he was anxious to get the ball rolling.

"What else do you need?" Jarrod diplomatically asked, trying to keep his temper at bay.

"I need for you both to trust me to do the job you've hired me to do. I have faced a hell of a lot worse than this when I was enlisted and I'm sure I will be able to get your girl back. I just need to ask a few more questions," Mike ordered. Jarrod nodded and sat back down behind his desk. Justin continued to pace the span of windows that covered the entire wall of Jarrod's office.

"Fire away," Jarrod offered, holding his arms wide.

"How exactly does this Jimmy character know Airiana?" Mike asked.

Jarrod sighed, hating that he was going to have to spill the ugly truth about Airiana's time in that God awful foster home. It wasn't his story to tell but it might be the only way to get her back. "His family housed foster kids and Airiana was one of them," Jarrod all but whispered.

"He fucking took advantage of her," Justin whispered. Mike's curt nod told him he completely understood Justin's meaning.

"I'll need the address for the family. With any luck, they are still in the same house and might have a lead as to where this Jimmy guy is," Mike said. He stood and turned to leave the office. "I don't have to remind either of you to let my team do the heavy lifting here, do I? You need to let me do my job and steer clear of playing the heroes. I'll find her and she'll be back here before you know it."

Jarrod nodded but made Mike no such promise. He knew if he or Justin got the chance to save their girl, they'd take it and to hell with their own personal safety. Airiana was theirs and he and Justin would do whatever it took to get her back, no matter the cost.

As soon as Mike left, Justin crossed the room to leave. "I've got to get out of this office," Justin complained. "Call me when you have news," he ordered and turned to walk out. Jarrod knew his brother was hurting, he just hated that Justin didn't turn to him. He hoped like hell Mike's promise came through because he had a feeling if they lost Airiana, he'd lose his brother too.

AIRIANA

A iri drifted between consciousness and a dream state for most of the day. The only way she could tell if it was nighttime or daytime was from the light coming from the room's only window. It was pitch black when she woke this time and she was relieved she was still alone. The last thing she remembered was Jimmy telling her he was going to go out to tie up a few loose ends. Airi panicked at the thought of those loose ends being her son or the guys but she also knew panicking wouldn't help her to find a way out of there. She was still so groggy and her head hurt like a son-of-a-bitch, reminding her she must have hit it at some point when Jimmy grabbed her in the alleyway behind the sub shop. Still, the only way she could remain so out of it was if Jimmy had drugged her and she wouldn't put it past him. She tugged at the handcuffs that bound her to the little metal bed and yelped at the pain that ratcheted through her wrists and down her arms. She stilled, trying to overcome the nausea she felt, willing herself to relax. She wanted to laugh at just how silly that thought was. How in the hell was she supposed to relax when she was being held captive by a mad man? He had killed Cole and probably others and Airi needed to remember she was dealing with a deranged murderer.

She let her eyes adjust to the darkness, trying to figure out just where it was he was holding her. The uncomfortable bed felt familiar. It was like the countless foster twin beds she was so grateful to sleep in night after night. If not for the families that took her in, she would have been in a group home and the stories she had heard about those were terrifying. She was thankful for every one of the families that took her in—well, except Jimmy's family. They turned a blind eye while their teenage son did unspeakable things to her. Even when the truth came out, and she proved she was pregnant, they denied the possibility of it being his baby. They had called her disgusting names and accused her of sleeping around, getting pregnant and then framing their son. Airi had felt so alone at that time. Not having anyone believe her or in her was the loneliest, lowest point of her life. It had taken her years to overcome her own insecurities and now, with Jarrod and Justin, she felt as though she had finally found her way.

Airi focused and concentrated on anything in the room that might give her a clue as to where she was being held. If she ever got her chance to escape, she would take it, and knowing where she was would give her a head start. She blinked against the darkness and realized she recognized the room she was in. If she wasn't mistaken, it was the room she shared with two other girls while she lived with Jimmy's family. The thought of him bringing her back to his childhood home made her sick but she'd expect no less from his crazy, twisted, skewed view of their time together.

She searched the room for anything that might help her but besides her bed and a small dresser, the place looked to be abandoned. There were no toys laying on the floor or clothes strewn across the furniture, as it was when she lived there. Three girls sharing a small room never allowed for things to be kept very tidy. In fact, the closet looked to be completely empty and the thought of the old house being left abandoned frightened her. If Jimmy had taken her to a place no one would think to look for her, what were her chances of escaping? She sobbed into the dark and realized she was completely alone in all of this. No one was there to comfort her, to take care of her or to rescue her. For the first time in almost two years since being found by her sister, Airi felt completely alone. She forgot how much she hated that feeling, especially after telling herself she would never be that girl again.

When Ivy and her husbands found her, she was a shy, timid, alone and afraid little girl. Airi was pregnant and had nowhere else to turn. When she finally started to get back on her feet, she promised herself and her unborn baby she would never go back to that life—that loneliness, ever. She had to raise her son and Airi never wanted Milo to look at her with the same damn pity she saw in stranger's eyes when she told them her story.

She wasn't a victim and she wouldn't start playing one now.

Jimmy had made one major miscalculation when he took her in that back alley. He thought he was kidnapping that same scared kid she used to be. He was wrong. She was a strong, capable woman now and she'd die before letting Jimmy just take what he wanted from her. She was going to show him just who she had become and hopefully, find her way back to her guys and Milo.

JUSTIN

Justin couldn't take the silence any longer. He had driven over to Ivy's place to pick up Milo. He needed to be close to Airi's son, needing some part of her to help him hold onto the hope she was going to be alright. But, every hour that ticked by made him more worried he was just being an optimistic fool.

"Hey," he groused when Holden answered the door. "I need to see Milo," he admitted. Holden's smile was forced and he stood out of the doorway, as if ushering Justin into their home.

"Thanks," he whispered, stepping into the entryway. Milo was standing by the television, watching some kid's cartoon and in his own little world. He had no clue his mother might not ever come back to them and Justin wished he could have that same ignorance. The pain of not having Airi close was eating at him, tearing his heart in two.

"We were taking bets on how long it would take you

guys to get here. I bet you'd get here first and well, I lost," Holden admitted. Justin realized what Holden had just said and looked around the house, knowing Jarrod had beaten him there.

"So, he's here then?" Justin asked.

"Yep, got here about an hour ago," Holden admitted. "Come on in the kitchen. Jarrod's talking to Slade and Ivy. Apparently, Ivy might know where that asshole has your girl." Justin's world seemed to rev up to full speed.

"How can Ivy know?" he questioned.

"Just come in the kitchen," Holden ordered. Justin grabbed Milo on his way into the bright, cheery kitchen, making him squeal by tickling his belly. God, he missed that kid. Milo patted his face, as if studying him and Justin playfully growled, pretending to eat the toddler's fingers. Milo yelped and giggled as Justin hugged him to his body.

"I missed you buddy," he whispered. Justin found Jarrod sitting in the corner of the room and Justin shot him an apologetic look.

"Don't," Jarrod said. "We'll talk about you walking out and leaving me alone in all of this later. Right now, I want to hear about Ivy's theory. You know where our girl is?" Justin didn't miss the way Ivy's face lit up when Jarrod referred to her sister as their girl. He wondered if she would be okay with them sharing Airi, even though Ivy lived that lifestyle herself. But, she was never anything but kind to either of them and now was no exception.

"Well, it's just an idea—a hunch really," she started.

"But has anyone thought to check the house where Jimmy grew up? After I aged out of the system, they moved Airi to another home, Jimmy's home. I lost touch with her and wasn't allowed any further contact or information since she was a minor. Does his family still live in the area?" She looked between him and Jarrod, as if they might have any answers.

Jarrod cleared his throat and Justin could tell he had gotten some news. "Our head of security called and said he had intel that place was abandoned. The family moved out of town not long after Airi had left them. No one has lived in that house for years." Justin felt angrier by the second but had to remember Milo wouldn't understand if he yelled at Jarrod. Having a toddler around had mellowed both of their tempers and he had to keep himself in check since the little guy was watching their every move.

"Mike called and you didn't let me know?" Justin asked. He tried to remain as calm as humanly possible but his words still came out as a heated accusation.

"You stormed out of my office, saying you couldn't take any more. I'm assuming you also turned your phone off?" Jarrod waited him out while he checked his cell phone.

"Shit," Justin grumbled when he realized he had set his phone to silent mode. He didn't hear the calls or texts that had come through from his brother. "Sorry, man. I must have hit it off when I got into the car. You're right—I just walked out on you and I'm sorry," Justin admitted. He felt like a first class ass for bailing on his brother that way. Airi was just as much Jarrod's and

Justin was acting as if he was the only person hurting from losing her.

"No more running, Justin," Jarrod ordered. "Whatever happens from here on out, we're a team." Justin nodded, knowing his brother was right.

"Got it," Justin agreed. Jarrod reached for Milo and the toddler willingly went to him.

"You know guys," Slade interrupted, "Just because a building seems empty, doesn't always mean it is. When I started renovating the club, I had to chase people out of there all the time. It was mostly homeless people just looking for a place to crash for the night but you never know. Maybe he'd think it's someplace no one would bother to look or maybe he'd just like the poetic justice of returning to the scene of the crime—who knows. It's worth checking it out though."

Jarrod looked at Justin and he could see the resolve in his brother's face. He thought Slade might be onto something too and there was no fucking way he'd let Jarrod go over to the old house alone.

"I'm going with you," Justin said. Jarrod smiled at him and Justin knew he had correctly guessed what his brother was thinking.

"You know that whole twin mind reading thing really freaks my sister out," Ivy teased. She took Milo from Jarrod and kissed her nephew's cheek. "Just find her and bring her home. Milo needs his mom and well, I need her too." Ivy's voice broke and Slade and Holden were immediately by her side, comforting her. Watching the three of them together nearly gutted

Justin, reminding him what he and his brother had possibly lost—what was taken from them.

"I'm going with you guys too," Holden admitted. He looked over to Ivy and Slade and they both nodded, giving him their silent support.

"Thanks, man," Justin said. "Call Mike and have him and some of his guys meet us over at the house. I have a feeling Ivy might be on to something," Justin ordered. Jarrod pulled out his phone and called Mike. Justin hoped like hell they were going to get a break. Not having Airi was tearing him apart minute by minute.

AIRIANA

Airi woke and this time the room was brighter from the sunlight that was filtering in through the curtains that covered the old windows. Her head was feeling a little better and she quickly searched the room for any sign of Jimmy. He never came back the night before and she really needed to use the bathroom and she was starving. A part of her worried something happened to him and he wasn't coming back. The panic of being chained to the bed and possibly having no one ever find her was terrifying.

"Hello," she shouted, hoping someone would be wandering by and hear her but she knew better than that. The house was abandoned and the chance of someone just passing by was slim to none. She shouted a few more times for good measure but her throat was dry and she had to stop shouting when her voice went hoarse.

The bedroom door burst open and Jimmy walked

in, a satisfied smirk on his face. "You called?" She was disgusted with herself for feeling even a twinge of relief at seeing him. But for now, he was her only hope of getting to the bathroom and stretching her aching body.

"Um, I have to pee," she whispered. Her voice was raspy from shouting.

Jimmy looked her body up and down, as if he didn't believe her and she almost found the whole thing funny. Who would lie about having to pee? Well, someone in her position, perhaps. Airi sighed, "It's been how many hours since you chained me to this bed? I have to use the bathroom, please," she begged. Jimmy seemed to enjoy toying with her and she knew she was going to have to lay it all out there for him.

"Or, I can just pee the bed and then you'll have to clean everything," she murmured. He seemed to consider her threat but finally gave in and pulled the key for the handcuffs from his pocket.

"Fine," he conceded. "But if you try anything I'll knock you out again." She pasted on her best fake smile and nodded.

"What exactly did you use on me?" she questioned. "I was out all night," she lied. She was awake for most of the night figuring out just where he had her stashed but she wouldn't tell him that. For all Jimmy knew she was still in the dark as to where he had taken her and she wanted to keep it that way. It gave her a fighting chance, knowing where they were and just how to get home from her current location. Jimmy didn't need to know she knew that.

"Oh, just a little roofie," he boasted.

She gasped, "You mean Rohypnol? As in the date rape drug?" Airi knew she couldn't be Jimmy's only conquest and knowing he had that drug in his possession only confirmed her worst fears—Jimmy was a predator.

"Yeah. It's good stuff, really. It turns women like you, the ones who don't want to be good girls and cooperate, into nice, obedient little girls." She felt sick thinking of how many times he had gone out on the prowl and roofied some poor, unsuspecting woman, only to drag her off to take advantage of her. He was disgusting and deserved to be behind bars.

Jimmy unlocked her hand cuffs and she sat up, testing to make sure she wasn't too lightheaded or sick from the after effects of the drug. Airi rubbed the feeling back into her numb arms. The pins and needles sensation quickly followed and hurt like hell but she would never tell Jimmy that. He would take some sick satisfaction in knowing he had caused her pain.

"I'll show you to the bathroom and then if you can behave you can have some food and water," he said. Her stomach growled at the mention of food and he smiled. "This way," he said. Airi stood and followed him down the hall, knowing just where she'd find the bathroom but playing along as if she had no clue. She felt weak and a little lightheaded but she kept that to herself too, steadying herself along the wall as she went.

"Where are we?" she asked. One thing she knew for certain about Jimmy was he liked the sound of his own voice. Airi knew if she could keep him talking it would give her time to re-group and hopefully figure out a plan to escape. Right now, she felt too weak to do anything of the sort, so getting Jimmy to ramble on about stuff was her best option.

"Well, that's need to know stuff and you don't need to know, darlin'." He chuckled at his own warped humor but she found him to be less funny. "This is the bathroom." He nodded to the door behind where they stood. "Leave the door cracked and don't do anything stupid, baby," he ordered. She nodded and went into the dirty bathroom. Airi flicked on the lights and realized the house had no power. She wondered if it even had running water but she didn't really care. She was so happy to use the bathroom, she didn't care if Jimmy stood on the other side of the door, peeping in on her like a disgusting pervert.

Airi finished up and tried to keep her temper in check. Her mouth, on the other hand, was going to be more of a challenge to control. "Enjoy the show?" she sassed on her way out of the bathroom.

"Always such a smart ass, Airi. I'll make sure you lose that character trait once I start training you to be more obedient. "Go back to the bedroom," he ordered. Her heart sank at the thought of having to go back to that small, dark bedroom. Her chances of finding a way out of the house would increase if he allowed her access to the kitchen. If she remembered correctly, there was a back door that led out to an alley that would take her to the main road. But Jimmy wasn't taking any chances.

She walked back to her bedroom and sat down on the bed. "How long are you going to keep me here?" she asked.

"As long as it takes for the two goons you're seeing to stop looking for you," he grouched. She smiled knowing Jarrod and Justin were looking for her. They must have been causing Jimmy some trouble if he was laying low to avoid them.

"Wipe the smirk off your face," he shouted. "You won't win. None of you will because it's my turn to win, Airi. I've been waiting too long to lose you to your rich, know-it-all boy toys." He sat down on the side of her bed and grabbed her wrist, pulling it up to the bedpost, cuffing it back into place. He left her right hand free and she must have looked confused as to why.

"I'm going to be generous and let you keep that one free to eat," he offered. "Start any shit and you'll have to figure out how to eat without your hands." Airi nodded. She was hungry enough to behave. Airi knew once she got some food into her system, she'd have more strength to put up a fight given the chance.

Jimmy pulled out a bag of fast food and handed her a breakfast sandwich. "Here," he offered. She snatched it out of his hand and pulled the sandwich free from the foil. "What, no thank you?" Airi snorted her disdain and shook her head.

"I don't think I'm feeling very grateful right now," she said around a mouthful of sandwich.

"You are an ungrateful bitch, always have been. I thought you'd show some appreciation for breakfast," he sulked. She wanted to laugh at the idea that she hurt his feelings. Honestly, she wanted to hurt a hell of a lot more than just his feelings.

"Sure, that's it—I'm ungrateful," she sassed. "I mean, how dare I not be grateful to you for kidnapping me and keeping me handcuffed to this bed all night?" Jimmy stood and threw the bag of fast food at her.

"You can fucking eat by yourself," Jimmy yelled. He turned to walk from the room and Airi didn't hide her laugh. Did he really think making her eat alone was hurting her? She welcomed not having to sit in the same space with him. Every minute she spent with Jimmy was a constant painful reminder of what he did to her. Eating alone was a reward but she'd keep that little bit of information to herself.

Jimmy stopped in the doorway and turned back to face her. "Oh, and don't get any ideas about trying to escape," he said. "I have the place rigged with explosives. You'll never make it out alive. If I can't have you, no one will. How poetic would that be? We can both die in the house where our love story began." Jimmy left the room, pulling her door shut behind him. Airi listened for him to lock the door but didn't hear anything. She wasn't sure if she believed Jimmy had explosives in the house. Was he crazy enough to want to blow himself up in the house with her? Airi knew he might be telling the truth but she also knew if she didn't do everything in her power to escape, she might never get the chance again. Sooner or later, Jimmy would have to move her. They couldn't stay in the abandoned house without electricity or water. If he didn't take her to another location, she might never get the chance to escape.

Airi was about halfway through her sandwich when she saw the small, shiny key sitting on the blanket next to her leg. She stretched and grabbed it trying to figure out if it was all just an elaborate trick Jimmy was playing on her. The key must have fallen out of his pocket when he stood to leave her room. Either way, she wasn't looking her gift horse in the mouth. She used her free hand to unlock the handcuffs and stood victoriously by the bed. Airi wanted to make a run for it but she knew she had to be smart. She didn't have a clue as to where Jimmy was in the house and knowing the floor plan wouldn't help her if he was close by. She knew of three exits to get out of that house. She used to escape that hell hole every chance she got when she was a teenager. Now would be no different, except this time she wasn't trying to sneak out of the house from her foster parents. Now, she was trying to escape their crazy son who wanted to hurt her or worse.

Airi gingerly opened the bedroom door and peeked out, finding no sign of Jimmy. She thought about it for a moment and decided not to go out through the kitchen. If he was finishing up his breakfast, he might be in the kitchen. Her best bet would be to go out through the front door and luckily for her, it was also the shortest route.

She crept down the hallway and just as she was about to make a break for the front entrance, she heard a loud crashing sound coming from the kitchen. It was now or never and Airi held her breath and made a run for it, not chancing a look back. Whatever was happening in the back of the house wasn't going to stop her from making her escape. She just hoped she could make it out of the house and back to the guys before Jimmy caught up with her.

JARROD

Justin looked just as anxious as Jarrod felt. They had parked around the corner from the address Ivy gave them and watched the abandoned building for hours. Just after the sun came up, a man matching Jimmy's description snuck into the house with a bag of what Jarrod assumed was fast food. If he was a betting man, he would guess the asshole had their girl tied up in that house and was bringing her some food. He had just left her there all night long, alone and that thought pissed him off. All that time they wasted watching the house, they could have just gone in there and possibly found Airiana.

Charging in now might put Airi's life in danger and Jarrod hated taking the chance. "Are we sure she's even in there?" he questioned Mike. His head of security shot him a look that was a cross between pity and disbelief.

"She's in there. One of my guys got close enough to

see in the house. He saw two figures moving around. One of them is a woman and I'm assuming it's Airiana." Jarrod knew Mike's guess was probably correct. Hell, he thought the only thing he could want in the world was to find Airiana. He didn't factor in the possibility of not being able to keep her safe if and when they did track her down.

"Don't worry Mr. Grayson, we'll take every precaution to get her out of there safely. My guys are moving in now," Mike assured. Jarrod just wished he shared the same confidence. He was sure he wouldn't be able to breathe again until he and Justin had Airiana safely back in their arms.

"Just get her back, Mike," Justin commanded. Mike nodded and left to meet up with the rest of his team. "So, we just sit here and wait?" Justin asked.

Jarrod flashed him a smile. "No fucking way," he growled. "How about you and I take the front of the house and go in to get our girl?" Justin nodded and they snuck from the truck to go to the front of the abandoned house and were just about knocked over when the front door swung open to reveal Airiana. Jarrod almost thought he was dreaming, seeing her standing there in the doorway.

"Airi," Justin yelled. She ran towards them and straight into their arms.

"Run," she shouted. "He has a bomb." Jarrod turned and started to run from the house, pulling Airiana along with him. He just hoped like hell Mike got to Jimmy before he could detonate the bomb.

"Get her to the car and I'll call Mike to warn him,"

Justin yelled. Jarrod wanted to tell his brother to forget it. There was no way he was going anywhere without him and from the determined look on Airiana's face, she felt the same way.

"You can't stay here," Airiana shouted. "Jimmy has the house rigged to explode. He doesn't care if he's caught in the crossfire. He said if he can't have me, no one will," she sobbed.

"Fuck," Justin swore, pulling out his cell. Jarrod knew his brother was doing the right thing. They had men in the house who needed to be warned but he wanted to tell his brother to keep moving.

"Get out now," Justin ordered. "He has a bomb."

Justin nodded and hung up his cell, pushing it back into his jacket pocket. "They have him," he said, smiling at Airiana.

"It can't be that easy," she cried. "He won't give up."

"Mike's on his way out now and he says they have Jimmy," Justin confirmed. Jarrod was feeling as skeptical as their girl but then Mike appeared in the front door of the old house, Jimmy in hand. Jarrod breathed a sigh of relief knowing this whole ordeal was about to be over. Everything around them seemed to slow down and time felt as though it stood still. Just when Jarrod thought they'd won, their world exploded into a shit storm around them and the house and all the men in it were gone. The last thing he remembered was seeing Airiana's beautiful face just before his world went dark.

JUSTIN

Justin sat by Airi's side, worried about Jarrod but knowing his brother would insist he be with their girl. He was pretty sure she had a broken arm and they were waiting for her to be taken up for x-rays. Jarrod didn't regain consciousness during the ambulance ride to the hospital. Justin knew that wasn't good but the EMT assured him it was typical for someone with possible head trauma. Jarrod was thrown the furthest in the blast and Justin worried he had some internal bleeding. He just wished he knew what to do but he was at a loss. His brother was the one who always had things under control, even when chaos reigned around them. Now, he had to keep it together for the three of them and get through the next few hours.

Justin could tell Airi was just as worried about Jarrod as he was. She must have asked him every other minute if he was going to be alright, despite her own obvious pain. He continued to assure her Jarrod was going to be just fine. He just hoped like hell he wasn't lying to her—Jarrod had to be alright, for all their sakes.

Justin called Ivy to let her know they had Airi and she was going to be fine. He explained they were waiting for x-rays and any news about Jarrod. Ivy wanted to come down to the hospital but Airi insisted she not bring Milo in to see her in that much distress. Ivy agreed and Justin promised to keep her in the loop.

Finally, after about forty minutes he couldn't sit around any longer. He needed news about his brother and doing nothing was killing him. "I'm going to go to the nurses station to ask about Jarrod," he said. Airi nodded and he could tell even that slight movement hurt her.

"Please, I'm dying not knowing if he's alright," she whispered. "If you can also ask the nurse when they will take me to x-ray, I'd appreciate it. The sooner we get my arm fixed up the sooner we can be with Jarrod." Justin stood and kissed her forehead. His own body felt as though it had been hit by a truck. When the EMTs insisted he get checked out, he baulked at the idea. He wanted them to help Jarrod and Airi but they kept pestering him to let them take a look at him, so he obliged. When they found nothing wrong with him, he grumbled something about them wasting time and demanded they get his brother and Airi to the hospital. He rode with Airi, deciding that was what Jarrod would want but he was torn. He wanted to believe if something horrible had happened to his brother he would have sensed it but Justin knew better than to believe in the hokey twin telepathy thing everyone accused them of having. Still, there was no one closer to him in the world than his twin brother and the thought of anything happening to Jarrod gutted him.

Justin found the head nurse on duty and basically begged her for any information she might have about his brother. The only news she had was they had taken Jarrod to surgery to stop the bleeding in his head. The apologetic look of pity she gave him didn't help Justin to feel any better.

"How about my girlfriend?" he whispered, trying to get his emotions under control. He needed to keep it together for Airi right now. "When will she be taken up for x-rays on her arm?"

"Right now," the nurse agreed. "I was just grabbing the forms that need to be filled out and then I can run her up." Justin nodded and thanked the nurse, following her back to Airi's cubicle.

Airi tried to sit up a little taller in bed and winced. "No, don't try to do that on your own," Justin scolded.

"You're not going to give me a moment's peace while I recover," she said, smiling up at him. "I'll be fine, Justin. It's Jarrod I'm worried about." Justin shot the nurse a look, hoping she'd get his silent message not to tell Airi about Jarrod. She had enough to worry about right now.

"No news yet, honey," Justin lied. "I'm sure they'll let us know something when there is news." The nurse followed his lead and kept her mouth shut, looking over the paperwork she had for Airi.

"I have all the information I need Miss Scott, from

when you were brought in. I just need to know if there is any chance you might be pregnant before I wheel you up to x-ray." The nurse looked expectantly at Airi, waiting for her to give some indication she wasn't pregnant and they could proceed with fixing her arm but Airi gave none.

"Airi?" Justin questioned. The look on her face was almost comical. In all of thirty seconds, Airi went from looking somewhat relieved the nurse was going to take her to x-ray, to looking like she smelled something rotten, to full on panic. She squinched up her cute button nose and a wave of panic washed over Justin too. Could she be pregnant? Jarrod and he hadn't really been cautious when it came to taking her. They both just assumed she had birth control covered, since she didn't insist they wear condoms. Still, they should have protected her and suited up but they were too in the moment to think clearly.

"Fuck," he swore when she didn't answer.

"Um," she nervously squeaked. "I missed a few pills when we were in Colorado. I talked to the pharmacist and he told me to just start the pack on the day I got them. But, now that you mention it, I am a couple weeks late. I thought it was just stress at first and with everything that happened in the last twenty-four hours, I just didn't think about it much."

"Fuck," Justin swore again.

"You keep saying that Justin but I didn't do it on purpose," she cried. He felt like a first class ass, making Airi cry right now. He gently wiped the tears that fell down her cheek with the back of his hand.

"I know, honey. It's not you I'm upset with. We should have protected you," he admitted.

"We?" the nurse looked him over but he just didn't give a fuck. He owed her no explanation and she wouldn't be getting one from him. "Um well, I'll have to get you to take a pregnancy test and if it's negative, we'll get you right up to have that arm looked at. If you are pregnant, we'll just have to take some extra precautions to protect the baby."

Hearing the nurse talk about a baby who may or may not exist did strange things to his heart. Justin wished like hell his brother was there because he would know exactly what to do but he would have to navigate this on his own. He wanted Airi and he was completely in love with her son. Milo had become a part of his everyday existence. The idea of having another baby in the house both excited and terrified him at the same time.

"You'll need to pee on this," the nurse said, handing Airi a pregnancy test. "The directions are on the outside package but if you need any help just holler." Airi nodded and took the test from the nurse.

"I've done this before. I have an almost two-year-old at home," she whispered.

"Well then, another little one shouldn't come as too much of a shock since you two have been through this before," the nurse said.

"Oh no, Justin isn't my son's father," Airi volunteered. He hated that she shared that news with the nurse. But more than her oversharing, he hated that Airi seemed almost put off by the thought of him being

Milo's dad. He'd give just about anything to be the little guys father. Justin knew he and Jarrod would be great dads to Milo and to their own baby when the time came. The question was—were they all ready for there to be a baby in the picture? Justin wasn't sure he knew the answer to that question but they were about to find out.

Airi stood and made her way over to the bathroom and looked back at him and smiled. "Wish me luck?" She asked. Justin tried to paste on his best smile, not sure if he was wishing her luck to be pregnant or not.

"Sure, honey," he offered. She nodded and disappeared into the adjoining bathroom. Minutes later, she came back into the tiny room and he was almost afraid to ask what the outcome was. She looked just as worried as he felt.

Airi looked him up and down and giggled. "You know it takes a few minutes until we get the results, right?" she asked.

"Sure," he lied. Airi's incredulous look told him she wasn't buying his assurances.

"What happens if it's positive?" she asked. The way her voice broke nearly did him in. He wanted to tell her they were going to get through this and everything was going to be all right but until he had news about his brother, he couldn't make her any of those promises.

"I don't know, Airi," he admitted. "We find our way forward, no matter what," he said.

"It's alright, Justin. You don't have to make me any promises. Not now, not with Jarrod—" her voice cracked again and this time, she didn't hide her sob.

"Aww, honey, don't," he said. Justin sat down next to her, the bed dipping with his weight. He was careful to avoid her bad arm, letting her body lean into his. It was the first time he chanced touching her since finding her earlier that day. Justin worried he wouldn't be able to take care of Airi or be everything she needed without his brother. He was wrong. He wanted her no matter what and she needed to hear that from him.

"If you're pregnant, I'll be the happiest man on the planet," Justin whispered. "I want everything with you, honey. We just need to get through this, one minute at a time, and then decide where we go from here. Nothing will change the fact that I love you, Airi—nothing." Her watery smile made him want to laugh, until her nurse came back into the room and didn't even bother to look at the two of them. She made a beeline for the bathroom and came back out with a triumphant smile on her face.

"Well, it looks like you two are going to have another little one under foot," the nurse said. Airi burst into tears and Justin had to admit he felt like doing the same. "I'll notify x-ray you are expecting and they will take good care of you," she offered. Airi sobbed and nodded and the nurse patted her leg on the way out of the room.

"I'm so sorry," she cried. "I never meant for any of this to happen, Justin."

"I know, honey but I'm not one fucking bit sorry. I'm happy we are going to have another baby. Hell, I'm in love with Milo and I already think of him as my own. I know Jarrod feels the same way about him," he said.

"He does?" Airi questioned.

"Yep," Justin said. "I see the way he is with Milo. He and I both are crazy in love with your son. Another baby will just mean more love to go around."

"We still have to tell Jarrod," she whispered.

"We will, honey. How about you get that arm taken care of and I go to find my brother. I won't share our news, we can do that together," he offered. Airi nodded and he stood to leave.

"I'll be back soon," he whispered and didn't turn to look back at her. He felt as though he wasn't being completely honest with Airi, not telling her about Jarrod being in surgery. He wouldn't needlessly worry her and until he had more information, he wouldn't tell her Jarrod was having brain surgery. It might cause her undue stress and now with the baby to consider he wouldn't risk it. He'd just have to come clean with Airi later when Jarrod was out of surgery and in recovery.

AIRIANA

Hours later, Airi sat with her arm freshly casted and was sure she was going to pass out from the pain. They had offered her something to take the edge off but she wouldn't take chances with the baby. From her doctor's guess she was about two months pregnant and taking anything might not be safe for her little one. This wasn't the first time she had a broken arm and she knew the pain might seem unbearable now but she'd feel better in a week or so. Her biggest worry right now was Jarrod and she couldn't help but think the worst had happened when Justin didn't return to check on her.

"You don't have to play the hero, you can have some Tylenol and the baby will be fine," the doctor offered. Airi knew she would function better if she wasn't in so much pain and she really wanted to go looking for Justin. She needed an update on Jarrod and she was sure Justin was keeping whatever was going on with him a secret. They both needed to realize she was a hell of a lot stronger than either of them gave her credit for.

"Fine," she finally conceded. "I'll take the medication, just to take the edge off."

"We'd also like to do a sonogram to make sure your baby is alright. The explosion threw you a good distance, Miss Scott. It might be better to be safe than sorry," he offered. She nodded, knowing he was right. Airi would have more piece of mind knowing the baby was doing well inside her. It was strange that just an hour ago she didn't even know of her baby's existence and now he or she was all Airi could think about.

"I'd like to wait until—um, well," she stuttered, not sure how to finish her sentence. What exactly did she call the guys, her bosses? She almost wanted to laugh at the thought. She decided to play it safe. "Until my boyfriend is available? I'd like to check on him. He was brought in the same time as me and we haven't had any word about him." The nurse shot Airi an apologetic look and her stomach dropped.

"What aren't you telling me?" she demanded.

"I told his brother he was taken into surgery a couple hours ago," the nurse admitted.

"Surgery?" Airi gasped. "What for?"

"Well, he had a brain bleed but they just sent down word he's out and it looks like he'll make a full recovery," she said. Airi stood, grabbing her things with her one good hand.

"Floor and room number please," she shouted. The nurse must have realized she wasn't going to concede and let them finish their exam. She needed to get to Jarrod and there would be no stopping her.

"Third floor, room three hundred and nine," she said.

Airi didn't wait for discharge papers or instructions. She made her way up to the third floor and found Jarrod's room number. She softly knocked on the door and then let herself in to find Justin sitting by Jarrod's bedside.

"How is he?" she asked. Justin shot her a sheepish look, quite like the one Milo gave her when he had been caught doing something wrong. "We'll talk about you keeping the truth from me later, Justin. Right now, I need to know how he is." She looked Jarrod up and down, noting how pale he was. He was so still and the machines around him beeped on. The side of his head was shaved and he had gauze that circled his head, much like a halo.

"The doctor said he'll be waking up soon but the surgery went well and it looks like he'll make a full recovery," Justin said. "How's the arm?" he questioned. She allowed him to pull her down onto his lap and wrap his arms around her body. She liked the way his hand laid protectively across her belly.

"Hurts," she admitted. "They gave me some Tylenol and said it would be safe for the baby," she whispered. "But they want to do a sonogram to make sure the he or she is alright in there."

Justin's whole body tense, "You mean there's a chance the baby is not okay?" he asked.

Jarrod popped an eye open and moaned. "You two

need to stop making so much fucking noise," he groaned. "And, what's all this talk about a baby?" Airi smiled at Justin and he shrugged.

"Sorry, man. We'll try to keep it down. The doctor said your head would hurt like a bitch when you woke up," Justin said.

"Well, the doctor was wrong," Jarrod whispered. "It hurts much worse than that." Jarrod opened both eyes and looked at Airi, noticing her cast.

He started to reach for her but groaned in pain. "No, don't move," Airi insisted. "You need to lay still."

"Your arm," he said.

"Yeah, it's broken. But, I'll be as good as new in about eight weeks," she said.

"Is Milo okay?" he asked.

Airi nodded, confused by his question. "Milo is fine. He's with Ivy and wasn't near the blast," she said.

"Well then what's all the talk about a baby?" Jarrod asked. Justin nodded at her and she suddenly felt nervous about telling Jarrod he was going to be a daddy.

"I found out downstairs—I'm pregnant," she admitted. It was hard to read Jarrod's expression. He was in so much pain she wasn't sure if he was hurting or upset about their news.

"How about I call the nurse in to give you some pain meds and we can talk about this later," Justin offered. Jarrod didn't answer and his brother left to find some help, leaving her alone with Jarrod.

"I'm going to be a dad?" he asked. Airi nodded.

"Yes," she said.

"Is the baby alright, you know from the explosion?" Jarrod asked.

"I don't know. They want to do a sonogram to check the baby out," she sobbed. What was it with her crying all the time? She wasn't so hormonal with Milo but she chalked it up to this being her third pregnancy.

The nurse and Jarrod's doctor entered the room to check on him. "How are you feeling?" the doctor asked.

"Like a mac truck tried to smash my head open," Jarrod grumbled.

"We are going to give you something to make you more comfortable," the doctor said. "You'll sleep for a bit but that will help. You're going to be here for a few days at least."

Airi stood from the side of Jarrod's bed, giving the doctor room to work and doubled over from the pains that shot through her abdomen. "Airiana," Jarrod shouted, trying to reach for her but Justin had her in his arms before she could hit the floor. He laid her in the empty bed next to Jarrod's.

"She's pregnant," Justin said. "They wanted to do a sonogram to make sure the explosion didn't hurt the baby but she refused."

"I wanted to wait for you two," she said through her gritted teeth. "What's wrong with my baby?" she questioned.

"I'll call for an OB consult but you should really be back in the emergency room," the doctor said. Both guys shouted a resounding "No" at the doctor's insistence and he finally gave in. "Fine, I'll have them bring the machine here and we can check the baby," he offered.

Airi nodded, holding her belly. "Hurry please," she begged. The thought of losing her baby consumed her. The pain felt very similar to when she lost her first baby—Jimmy's baby. She thought about how he would find it to be some sick poetic justice she would miscarry Jarrod and Justin's child because of his handy work. She wouldn't be able to live with herself if she lost the baby but waiting and worrying was all she could do now.

———

It felt like an eternity had passed for the OB doctor on duty to show up with a sonogram machine to check her. The sharp, stabbing pain had subsided and she was feeling much better. She hated that she had caused such a scene but she wasn't taking any chances with the baby. Jarrod seemed more relaxed since taking his pain medication but he refused to sleep until he knew she was alright. She still didn't know how Jarrod felt about her news and honestly she was too afraid to ask. First, she needed to make sure her baby was alright, then she'd worry about how the guys felt about her pregnancy.

"This will be a little cold," the technician said, spreading the gel on her lower abdomen. The doctor started firing off questions but all she could do was hold her breath and wait for the swooshing sound that always comforted her when she heard Milo's heartbeat. When the tech finally found the baby's heartbeat and that glorious sound filled the room, she breathed a sigh of relief. The guys seemed even more confused until the doctor assure them the baby's heartbeat was supposed to beat that fast. The technician worked on getting a visual of the baby and the doctor smiled at the computer screen.

"Your babies look wonderful," he soothed.

"Oh thank God," she said. "I was so worried."

"Wait—babies?" Justin asked. Airi did a double take at the screen, realizing just what she had missed seconds earlier. There were two babies inside of her.

"Two?" she questioned. The doctor continued to smile and nod, looking over to Jarrod and Justin.

"I'm assuming one of you is the father. And I'm also guessing you are twins, so it's not too far-fetched." Airi didn't answer the doctor, not sure how to explain she was in a threesome and technically only one of her guys was the father. How exactly was she supposed to explain what the three of them had come to mean to each other or what they had surprisingly created together.

"I'm recommending you spend a week on bed rest, Miss Scott," the doctor ordered. "In fact, given the trauma your body has been through, I'm going to admit you and advise that you don't move from this bed." Justin smiled at her and then Jarrod. He was going to let them all stay together and that was just what she needed right now.

"Thank you," Justin said. "I'll make sure she stays in

this bed, even if I have to tie her down." Justin shot her a wolfish grin and bobbed his eyebrows.

Jarrod groaned from his bed and Airi looked over to make sure he was alright. "I'm pretty sure that's how she got pregnant in the first place," he moaned. They laughed and the doctor gave her a few more instructions before he left, assuring her that her babies were in good hands. Airi just needed rest and that sounded absolutely perfect to her and when they were all up for it, they would have a nice long talk about what was going to happen next. She had been a single mother for so long she was used to making her own decisions but this time would be different. This time, she would have two men she adored taking care of her and that was more than she could ever wish for.

JARROD

I t had been a week and Jarrod was thrilled he and Airi were finally getting sprung from the hospital. He couldn't wait to get home to Milo and start their lives together. The police detective who was handling the case had been by earlier that morning to confirm Jimmy had died in the explosion. Unfortunately, the detective also said that Mike and two guys from their private security team also died in the blast. Jarrod worried Airi would blame herself for their deaths until the detective told them about the note he found in Jimmy's apartment. It was basically a suicide note that spelled out his plans, tying the case up in a neat package. Jimmy had planned on luring the guys and Milo over to the abandoned house and ending them all with his homemade bomb but the guys showing up with the police kind of put a kink in his plot. Jimmy must have thought that having Jarrod and Justin there would be enough and set the bomb off. Luckily for them, Airiana had found a way to escape and they were mostly clear of the blast zone when he detonated the bomb. For the most part, Jarrod felt damn lucky. He was walking out of that hospital with the woman he loved, his brother, Milo and the promise of two new lives they created. Lucky didn't even begin to cover how he was feeling.

They really hadn't talked much about the newest additions to their family. He and Justin had a few quiet conversations while Airiana was sleeping but for the most part they both agreed they were thrilled about the babies. They just wanted to make sure Airiana and the twins were alright before he and Justin went full throttle making plans for their new family. Their priority was getting everyone healthy enough to leave the hospital, the rest would fall into place. Plus, their hospital stay gave Justin time to get everything ready for their special surprise.

After they had been home two days, they both decided it was time to show Airiana just how excited they were about the two new additions to their family. Justin was holding down the fort at work, allowing Jarrod to work from home to finish recovering. It also allowed him to keep an eye on Airiana. They allowed her to work from home but the doctor said she had to take it easy for a few more weeks until she was into her second trimester. Jarrod had been medically cleared to go back to work but they decided to keep that little bit of information to themselves. If Airiana knew, she'd be less likely to follow doctor's orders and they weren't willing to take any chances with her or the babies.

He walked into the room the three of them shared,

fresh from the shower. He liked the way Airiana looked him over, her eyes lingering where his towel was wrapped just below his waistline. "Don't look at me like that," he growled. "We both know you can't do anything about it." Airiana's pout nearly had him caving. As soon as the doctor gave them the green light, he couldn't wait to give her everything she craved and more.

"These next few weeks better fly by," Airiana groused. "My hormones are out of whack and I'm horny." Jarrod's laugh seemed to pissed her off more and she crossed her arms over her impressive cleavage. Jarrod loved how her curves were fuller now with the pregnancy. He couldn't wait to learn every one of Airiana's new curves by heart.

"How about you let us surprise you tonight? Justin and I have a nice, quiet dinner planned." Airiana seemed to perk up at the mention of food, causing him to chuckle again.

"Well, if sex is completely off the table..." she teased.

"It is," he confirmed.

"Then fine, I could eat." Her matter of fact declaration had him full on belly laughing. His girl was always up for food, now more than ever.

"Any cravings?" he questioned.

"Yep—tacos and ice cream," she said. Judging from her giggle, he must have made a face. The idea of having tacos and ice cream together disgusted him.

"Okay baby, tacos and ice cream it is," he agreed. Airiana squealed and clapped at his compliance. Jarrod quickly dressed and gave an order for her to rest and be ready for dinner by six. He and Justin were going to give their girl the surprise of her life and he just hoped like hell she'd say yes.

———

Justin got home with bags of takeout from Airiana's favorite Mexican place just as Jarrod was setting the table. "Hey, perfect timing," Jarrod drawled. "Ivy was just here to pick up Milo and we have our girl all to ourselves."

"Yeah, they were a little backed up at the restaurant," Justin said. "How's our girl?"

"She's fine. Stubborn but good. She actually undressed me today," Jarrod teased. "With her eyes," he quickly added when he saw the flash of anger in Justin's eyes. Jarrod knew his brother had to be on edge with holding down the fort at home and dealing with the news of the babies.

"Not funny, man," Justin said.

"Okay, I can see you aren't in the mood for jokes yet. I understand—it's too soon. I decided I'm coming back to work on Monday," he said. Justin looked him up and down, as if trying to decide if he agreed with his decision or not.

"Is that a good idea?" he asked. Jarrod loved the way Justin seemed to want to protect both him and Ariana but Jarrod knew it was time to start picking up some of the slack.

"Yeah," he said. "I'm more than ready. I've been staying home to keep an eye on Ariana but she's only on half-day bed rest now. I think we can make sure our girl behaves for two weeks until the second trimester starts."

"I'll behave," she agreed. Airiana was standing behind him. "I would never do anything to hurt our babies," she said, gently cupping her tummy. "I love them just as much as I love the two of you." Jarrod and Justin flanked her sides and wrapped her in their arms. Justin smiled at him and he knew exactly what his brother was silently trying to tell him. It was time to give Airiana their surprise.

Jarrod felt his heart racing, worried about all the possibilities the next few minutes would bring but he would only accept one outcome—Airiana saying yes to being theirs forever.

"Marry us," Justin whispered. He pulled the ring from his pocket and held it up for her. Jarrod could tell his brother was just as nervous as he was. "Be our wife, Airi," Justin asked.

Jarrod took the ring from his brother and slipped it onto Airiana's finger, noting it fit perfectly, just the way she did between the two of them. "Please, Airiana," Jarrod begged. "Say yes." Airiana looked between the two of them, tears streaming down her beautiful face and Jarrod knew she was about to make all their dreams come true.

"Yes," she breathed. "I'll marry you both."

"Thank fuck," Justin exhaled. "I thought my heart was going to beat out of my fucking chest," he admitted.

"We have one other question, baby," Jarrod murmured. Airiana looked at him expectantly and he couldn't help himself, he dipped his head to kiss her lips. "Let us adopt Milo. He's already ours and we both want to be his dads." Airiana nodded, overcome by her emotions.

"I'd love that and so would he," she cried.

Jarrod held Airiana in his arms, encircling her body with Justin's and he knew they had found their perfect match. She was not only their personal assistant but the love of their lives—their future, their everything, theirs.

EPILOGUE

ELLIOTT

Elliott Hale had spent the better part of a day hiking up the mountain outside of town and she was about ready to turn around and hike back down. She wanted to laugh at herself, because she knew that wasn't an option. Really, her only hope was to find Nash Lewis but she also knew he might turn her away once she found him. They hadn't left things between them on the best of terms when he left.

Really, Ellie couldn't blame him for being angry with her still, she acted like a child when he announced he was going to take some time for himself and go off grid. Nash decided to move up to his cabin on the top of the mountain in the middle of nowhere and Ellie worried she would never see him again. Her fears were silly really, they had been best friends since she could remember and she should have known better.

Despite his anger over her throwing a fit when he left, instead of a going away party, Nash had checked in with her weekly. It was usually by text but she was grateful for every message that told her he was alive and well. And, for the most part, her life had continued back in town, sans one best friend but she was miserable without him—not that she would admit that to him.

She was a criminal defense lawyer and damn good at her job, even if she did say so herself. She represented some high profile cases in her almost ten years of practicing law but the one she was on now was the worst. She had the distinct displeasure of representing William Keller and if she had to guess, he was the trouble that was following her. Well, the person he hired to go after her, since he was still safely tucked away in his jail cell last time she checked.

Keller was doing time for human trafficking and had hired her firm to prove his innocence. Since she was not a partner in the firm, the unwanted caseloads had often trickled down to her and she was the unlucky recipient of Keller's case. She was sure he was guilty, and even asked to be recused from the case but the judge refused telling her to just do her job. When she had to face Keller alone again at the penitentiary to go over a few details, he told her he was informed she asked to be taken off his case. The only way he would have found that out was from the judge and that told Ellie all she needed to know—she was in way over her head. Keller's threat was overkill, she knew exactly what was going to happen to her if she didn't win his case. Ellie also knew what could potentially happen to thousands of women and children if she did win the case and she wasn't sure which would be a worse outcome.

When she got home that evening to find her place had been broken into and vandalized, she knew calling the local police would be pointless. She had a feeling the case was bigger than just her involvement and she worried Keller and his business associates would have more than just a dirty judge on their payroll. The only person she could think to turn to was Nash. She ditched her phone, knowing it was probably bugged and packed her backpack, only to disappear into the woods that joined her little town and the mountain that her best friend lived atop. Ellie wasn't being overly dramatic when she thought of Nash being her only hope—he was just that. Ellie just hoped she could get to him before whoever was threatening her caught up to her.

WEST

J ake Weston knew he was taking a chance tracking Elliott Hale up the mountain when he had no idea where she was headed. He knew Miss Hale was heading into visit Keller and he took his chance to search her home but she came back before he could finish and he had no choice but to hide out and then follow her up that damn mountain. What he really wanted was his nice warm bed and possibly a beer or two but that wasn't going to happen any time soon. The FBI didn't give a fuck about what he wanted or his own comfort. They wanted information on Keller and if his hunch was correct, Elliott Hale knew a hell of a lot more than she was letting on.

Once he realized she was leaving, sneaking up one of the trails that would lead her by foot out of town, he had no other choice but to leave his warm car and follow her. The problem was he wasn't dressed for the impending storm as she was. West was freezing his ass off and he hoped she'd either get to where she was going soon or turn around and hike back to town. The last thing he wanted to do was wait out the snowstorm that was raging on around him. Near whiteout conditions were making it too damn hard to continue but he also knew turning back wouldn't be any easier. His only option was to hope Miss Hale knew where she was going or he could come up with a fucking good excuse as to why he was trailing her.

West had managed to stay back out of eyesight but he worried if the snow kept coming down, his dark jacket was going to give him away. He stuck out like a sore thumb and every time Elliott Hale turned around, he was sure she was going to see him. His feet were freezing since the trail was completely covered by at least a few inches of snow that had quickly fallen. West stumbled forward, tripping over a rock and tumbling down to the ground. He laid there for a minute, hoping he didn't make enough of a ruckus to warrant attention. Just when he thought it was safe to get up, Elliott Hale stood over him and he knew his cover had been blown. It was fight or flight time and with the way his ankle throbbed, he was pretty sure neither would work well in his favor.

"Oh my goodness, are you alright?" she gushed. West tried to nod and wave her attentions off but he failed miserably. Instead the pretty brunette had her arms around him, trying to help him up from the cold, wet ground.

"I'm fine," he said, even though his fucking ankle screamed otherwise. "I was just out hiking and this storm came out of nowhere. I'm afraid I'm not really dressed for a snowstorm," he covered. "I was trying to make it down the mountain but I got turned around and now I'm afraid I'm lost."

"My friend's cabin is up the path just a little further," she offered. "Do you think you can make it?" The idea of getting close to Elliott Hale would make his job a whole lot easier. But he also stood the chance of blowing his cover if he was discovered. From everything he knew about Elliott Hale, she was smart and he didn't want to take a chance she'd figure everything out.

The wind picked up around them, reminding West he had two choices—go with Miss Hale or stay on the side of the mountain and probably die. Either way was a risk but at least he'd have a fighting chance if he let her help him. Besides, judging from the determined look on her pretty face, there was no way she was about to leave him on the trail.

"I can make it," he said. "Thank you." She pulled his arm around her neck and he held onto her as if she was his lifeline.

"I'm Elliott Hale, by the way," she yelled over the howling winds. "But everyone calls me Ellie."

"Jake Weston but you can call me West," he offered. He learned from years of having secrets with the FBI to tell as many truths as possible so you don't get caught up in the lies. His name was probably the only truth he was going to be able to give to Elliott but that was the nature of his work. Until he could find out just where she stood with Keller, he needed to be careful and lying to his rescuer was his only option.

NASH

Nash finished chopping the load of wood and carried it to his porch to stack. It felt like snow and he was happy for the change in weather. It had been a warmer than usual fall and he was hoping the snow would keep some of the nosey townies away. They were constantly hiking up his mountain and stumbling across his little cabin. He was ready for some true solitude and he was hoping the impending storm might give him just that.

After working all day to get ready for the snow, he decided to take a quick shower to warm up and then he'd make himself a steak for dinner—he had earned it. He was just about to sit down to dinner when a quiet rapping at the door had the hairs on his neck standing on end. It had just started snowing and Nash was sure he'd be stuck with whoever had the misfortune of knocking on his door. There was no fucking way he'd want to entertain a visitor until the storm passed. Mountain snow tended to linger and be harder to get

through than the stuff they got down in town. The way
the storm raged on outside of his cabin, this snow was
going to make getting back down the mountain damn
near impossible.

The second knock at the door was a lot louder and
more insistent, telling him whoever was on the other
side of the door wasn't going to just give up and leave.
"I'm coming," he growled. He pulled the cabin door
open to reveal two figures standing on the other side
and from the looks of them, they were freezing. The
wind blew in a good deal of snow and made it near
impossible to see who the people were.

"Come in," he yelled into the winds. The two
people entered his cabin and he used all his body
weight to push the front door closed again.

The smaller figure pulled her scarf free from her
face and he'd know those eyes anywhere—Ellie. "Fuck
Ellie, what are you doing out in this storm?" She smiled
up at him, her cheeks bright red from the cold air and
snow that pelted her face.

Her smile was quickly replaced with worry and he
pulled her in for a hug. "I need your help," she
whispered against his neck.

"Anything," he breathed.

She looked at the man who had pulled his jacket
from around his face and shook her head. "Not now—
later. We can catch up later and I'll fill you in about
everything," she said. Her smile was back in place but
Nash knew Ellie well enough to know that something
was bothering her.

"This is West," she offered. "I found him on the

mountain on my way up here. He apparently twisted his ankle when he tripped over a rock."

Nash shot Ellie a disapproving look, "You just picked up a complete stranger and brought him up to my cabin?" Nash questioned.

Ellie's mouth gaped open, "You would have had me leave him there? He wasn't dressed for the storm and I am not the kind of person to just leave someone to die, Nash Lewis." The way she chided him made him want to laugh. His Ellie was always a spit fire but when she scolded him, it made him a little hot—though he'd never tell her that.

"No, you aren't, Ellie girl. You are the sweetest most caring person I know—sometimes to a fault," Nash said.

West held up his hands, as if in defense. "I'm not here to cause any trouble. I fell and Ellie was nice enough to save my ass. End of story. As soon as this storm is over, I can call for some help and be on my way," he offered. Nash gave a curt nod, knowing there were no other options. With the storm, they had no cell service. He could radio for help but help wouldn't be able to get to them before the storm broke.

"It's fine," Nash lied. "I've known Ellie a damn long time and there is no way she would have left you on the side of the mountain to die. It's just not in her."

Nash noted the skepticism in West's eyes, "Seems that way," he agreed. "Anyway, I'm thankful—to you both."

"No problem. Let's get you off that ankle and I'll find you both some dry clothes and something to eat,"

Nash offered, helping Ellie off with her coat. It had been almost a year since he saw her and his traitor's body still responded to her the way it always had. He needed to remind himself of all the reasons why the two of them just wouldn't work—the first and most pressing reason being his PTSD. She wasn't a good idea, not since he was discharged from the Air Force, for reasons he didn't like talking about, not even to his best friend.

"Thank you, Nash," she whispered.

"You never have to thank me, Ellie. I would do anything for you," he admitted.

"Well, just about anything," she corrected and winked up at him. He wanted to chuckle but there was nothing funny about having the woman he loved in his cabin and not being able to take what he wanted from her.

"Yeah, just not that, Ellie," he whispered as he walked into his bedroom. He knew she could hear him from her little gasp but he didn't turn around, not wanting to see the hurt and disappointment on her face. Because the one thing he couldn't do for her was love her—that would just be too much.

The End

**Double Crossed (Taken Book 2) coming soon!

ABOUT K.L. RAMSEY

Romance Rebel fighting for Happily Ever After!

K. L. Ramsey currently resides in West Virginia (Go Mountaineers!). In her spare time, she likes to read romance novels, go to WVU football games and attend book club (aka-drink wine) with girlfriends.

K. L. enjoys writing Contemporary Romance, Erotic Romance, and Sexy Ménage! She loves to write strong, capable women and bossy, hot as hell alphas, who fall ass over tea kettle for them. And of course, her stories always have a happy ending.

K.L. Ramsey's social media links:

Facebook
https://www.facebook.com/kl.ramsey.58
(OR)
https://www.facebook.com/k.l.ramseyauthor/

Twitter

https://twitter.com/KLRamsey5

Instagram
https://www.instagram.com/itsprivate2/

Pinterest
https://www.pinterest.com/klramsey6234/

Goodreads
https://www.goodreads.com/author/show/
17733274.K_L_Ramsey

Book Bub
https://www.bookbub.com/profile/k-l-ramsey

Amazon.com
https://www.amazon.com/K.L.-Ramsey/e/B0799P6JGJ/

Ramsey's Rebels
https://www.facebook.com/groups/ramseysrebels/

Website
https://klramsey.wixsite.com/mysite

KL Ramsey ARC Team
https://www.facebook.com/groups/klramseyarcteam/

KL Ramsey Street Team
https://www.facebook.com/
groups/ramseyrebelsstreetteam/

Newsletter
https://mailchi.mp/4e73ed1b04b9/authorklramsey

MORE WORKS BY K.L. RAMSEY

The Relinquished Series

Love Times Infinity

Love's Patient Journey

Love's Design

Love's Promise

Harvest Ridge Series

Worth the Wait

The Christmas Wedding

Line of Fire

Torn Devotion

Fighting for Justice

Last First Kiss Series

Theirs to Keep

Theirs to Love

Theirs to Have

Theirs to Take

Second Chance Summer Series

True North

The Wrong Mr. Right

Ties That Bind Series

Saving Valentine

Blurred Lines

Taken Series

Double Bossed

Double Crossed

Coming Soon:

Alphas in Uniform

Burn for Me

Owned

His Secret Submissive

Made in United States
North Haven, CT
30 September 2021